THE HARD LIFE OF A STONE

and Other Thoughts

I0563861

MARVIN COHEN

Edited by Colin Myers

Sagging Meniscus

Set in Mrs Eaves XL with LaTeX.

ISBN: 978-1-952386-10-7 (paperback)
ISBN: 978-1-952386-11-4 (ebook)
Library of Congress Control Number: 2021942451

Sagging Meniscus Press
Montclair, New Jersey
saggingmeniscus.com

Publication History

— Marvin's self-portrait comes from *Self Portrait—Book People Picture Themselves*, 1976, edited by Burt Britton. Note: "Cohen attended Cooper Union to pursue the study of art seriously; seriously, that is, until the day he found himself writing in his art classes instead of doing his art assignments." (*Bay News*, Sept 11th, 1978)

— "All The World's A Pun" was hand-printed by Louisa Scioscia Stephens, Marvin's "favorite typographer."

— "A Tale of Years" is an undated broadsheet; no publication details known.

— "Game of All-Playful Sport" is an undated poem found loosely inserted in a copy of *How the Snake Emerged from the Bamboo Pole but Man Emerged from Both*.

— Episodes from "Blat's Tales" appeared in *Ambit #49*, 1971, and *Center #7*, 1975.

— "Time and Eternity" appeared in *Ambit #57*, 1974; it's a version of a talk given at the London Southbank Poetry International Festival, Summer 1973.

— "Time's Journey Through Immortality" appeared in *Antaeus #10*, 1973.

— "Early Lessons In Knowing Your Place" appeared in *Ararat #38*, 1969.

— "A Rumination On The Distance Of Travel" appeared in *Ararat #61*, 1975.

— "Three Outbursts Of Time" appeared in *The Avant-Garde Today*, 1981.

— "Inside The Head That's Inside The Head" appeared in *Breakthrough Fictioneers*, 1973.

— "If What's Written Become True" appeared in *Handbook #1*, 1977.

— "A Fable With A Still Moral" appeared in *Hesitant Wolf & Scrupulous Fox*, 1973.

— "How To Counter Time's Speed" and "Time Brought To A Head" appeared in *Monks Pond #4*, 1968.

— The Afterword is from William Smart's memoir in *Mt San Angelo*, 1984.

Quoted in the Preface:

— The cited dedication is in Susanne Ostro's copy of *The Inconvenience of Living*.

— "The Drumbeat of Society," (Nina Buckless) in *fictionwritersreview.com*, 2017.

— "An Unnecessary Autobiographical Pre-Beginning" in *Plays from the New York Shakespeare Festival*, 1986.

— "Originalities" (B.S. Johnson) in *New Statesman*, November 17th 1967.

— "Marvin Cohen joins the Carriage House Series" in *Westfield Record Press*, April 20th, 2006.

The following episodes were read by Marvin Cohen and Wallace Shawn at *Poets at the Public*, a performance at the New York Public Theater, Dec. 4th, 1978, featuring works by Marvin Cohen and David Mamet:

— "Reality Blots Out Life"
— "Time's Journey Through Immortality"
— "Once or Twice"
— "Inside the Head That's Inside the Head"
— "Thunder Breaking in on Sleep"
— "Within the World, There's Me"
— "Ideas Are Mental Versions of the Outer World"

PREFACE

This anthology is about perception: of the awareness of existence and experience; of reality and truth; and the relativity of time and place. This theme is recurrent in Marvin Cohen's work, for example in his 1982 collection: *Aesthetics in Life and Art, Existence in Function and Essence and Whatever Else is Important Too* and in his recommendations for Antaeus magazine's 'Neglected Books' feature: Henri Bergson's *Creative Evolution*, and Theodor Adorno's *Negative Dialectics* and *The Jargon of Authenticity*.*

Most of the contents are drawn from Marvin Cohen's big box of previously unpublished typescripts ranging from the 1960s to the 1980s and the rest from published but unanthologized work. Its title is borrowed from a promised but unrealized 1975 Capra Press collection. Though it has taken a long time to see print, the book is remarkably unanchored in time or place. As Marvin writes in a book dedication:

> "To . . . who, though they happen to reside at Upper West Side nevertheless it's only an accident that they live there, but a long confirmed and substantiated and now custom-upheld one. But what's a place? A place is only something in time. And what's time? Time is us—each person."

Of his work in general, Marvin has said: "The subject that has most absorbed me is the emotional psychology and philosophy of my fellow human beings (a comparative mirror and index or reference to myself) . . . and all things that count in

---

*"Neglected Books of the Twentieth Century," *Antaeus #18*, 1975

the wild aggregate of piecemeal miscellaneousness that we narrow off into 'character' and 'personality'." *[Westfield Record Press, 2006]*

"I've been trying to figure out . . . what makes people [want] and then their *learning not to want* when such wanting is shown to be of no avail, or no longer of any avail; and their developing new wants that do have more probable hopeful possibilities of getting themselves, by the outside world of mainly people but including one's body itself, co-operated with." *[Necessary Ends, 1986]*

Though often serious in theme, Marvin's writing is seldom serious in tone: "I've always been humorous. I've always had a funny bone. Entertaining people. Some aesthetic philosophers say that 'creativity is play.' You are at liberty to make any sequence of words any way you want. And you take the responsibilities of how people are going to react. But in being playful, successfully playful, other people may be grateful that you have given them an occasion of humor." *[The Drumbeat of Society, 2017]*

B.S. Johnson, the English experimental novelist, suggested that readers might benefit by reading Marvin "in fragments, perhaps choosing at random a section long enough to read between tube stations, or between going to bed and falling asleep. Marvin Cohen would presumably be delighted that they had thus entered into the spirit of the thing." *[New Statesman, 1967]*

—Colin Myers

Reality Checklist

Reality & Truth

Time & Place

Marvin Cohen: Self Portrait

THE HARD LIFE OF A STONE

Existence & Experience

THE HARD LIFE OF A STONE
(OR, HOW TO GET THERE: A MOVING TALE OF GETTING OFF AT YOUR STATIONARY STOP)

By Marvin Rockbottom Cohen, The Pebble's Poet, Whose Prose Moves Mountains Into Summits Of Prayer And Layers Of Repose.

What are you doing?

Resisting inertia.

Why all that bother?

You think inertia is *easy* to resist? It's tempting me to become a stone. Not a *cabbage* (which takes the trouble to breathe), but a *stone!*

Oh. But don't you like to move?

Stop animating me! Of *course* I don't! My tendency is that of a *slug*, which I emulate indifferently.

You seem to lack enterprise, and ambition.

Idle goals; when my *true* goal is idleness.

Why do you aspire so *inactively*?

To attain quiescence, and some modicum of repose.

You have no get-up-and-go! What you lack is *dash!*

What *you* see as a *fault*, *I* find virtuous. I incline toward *peace*. Why disturb my pacifist ideal?

Passivity cheats the human condition. The way we were constructed, it means we've got to *move*. Otherwise, we insult ourselves with negation and death.

That's a very lively argument you have. But it doesn't *move* me.

(Incredulously:) Do you find sloth comfortable!?

Yes. It's so restful.

(Concerned:) Have you had your health examined lately?

Yes, but it's not good for my *body*, which likes to observe the *passive* state.

If you merely *vegetate*, can you call yourself human?

(Unperturbed:) I aspire to the *non*-human. A *stone* suits me best.

Then were you born a pebble?

A timid one. But soon I gained courage, and became a little bo(u)lder.

You're making a mountain out of nothing.

(Ecstatically:) A *mountain*! Ah that's the *pinnacle* of my ideals! An ascendancy of inaccessibility! The *summit* of buried dreams. *(Disconsolately:)* Alas, it's just not in the picture, where *my* horizon is concerned!

(Encouragingly:) Perk up, my lowly one. If your destiny is stone-like, be a *lively* stone, at least.

(Dreamlike:) My ideal environment as a stone would be plenty of moss.

Yes, you'd roll your own. But that's no fun.

No; it's *fung*us.

Oh. Is it fun-to-be-gas?

No. That's too vapid for me, as well as rapid. A stone, having nowhere to go, gathers a monumental solidity: more durable than any inflated gust of dust.

But vapor is capable of a higher *dreaming* substance.

What I like is more elemental. It's *down-to-earth* for me. The clouds were never my destiny. I tend to *gravitate*; so levitation must take wing and fly out of my life. I like to get down to the rock bottom of things. That's where the *real truths matter*.

Rock bottom! And *yourself* be a rock?

Well, a *stone*, for modesty. I wouldn't claim more than that, nor *rock* my foundations too *hard*.

No; nothing earthshaking: right?

Right. Ultimately a stone's repose is all the square inch I could wish for. *(Confidingly:)* I do have one ambition: to settle down.

That's an upstanding conservative aspiration. You want to get established?

Yes. And go no further than my own roots.

(Disparagingly:) That's not very *far*.

No. Motion defies solidity. A thing is solid while, or if, it stands still. A stationary thing *exists*. But not a *moving* thing.

To go against motion is to court death.

There's *peace* in death. It attracts me.

There's no *vitality* in your longing.

It falls *short* of *long*ing.

(Trying to rally other:) Come on now! More zip and pep!

It's no use. Being dynamic is for less lazy people. Give me inertia, and I reside contentedly in its steady dependability of earth. Let the moon and stars go rocketing along, and other frail loops of news go flying by. For all their trouble, they don't amuse me. Relativity is not for me. The more minimum something is, the more perfectly absolute it is. Why be motivated? Better just *be*: there's greater *substance* in it.

Is that, *substantially*, your doctrine?

Insofar that I *reside* in it. There's no waste.

Ah, that's very economical of you.

Yes. A stone doesn't waste anything.

Not *geting* anywhere, it has no product to waste.

(Agreeing:) No. I call that *perfection*.

And I, *death*.

I want to *inert*.

Yes: *in earth*.

A stone is earth's kin. I repose in my family bosom.

A stone is what tombs are made of.

(Baiting:) Granted—I mean granite. Grand, isn't it?

A stone doesn't speak. I'm silent.

But you've been speaking all this while—all to wile me?

I was, so to speak, an *apprentice* stone. Now I'm a *journeyman* one.

Your *journey* from *man* is over, and you're stone cold?

I'm cold to what you say, and stone-deaf, too,

Oh; how unheeding of you.

Ultimately, I've become inert.

Rest in peace.

I'll rest—as an earthpiece.

Have you become arrested?

Yes: A stone's development is no more.

Then I'll quarry you no more.

My motion is ceased.

And your notion, diseased.

And my earth-plot, leased.

(An inert curtain begins to fall. But motion gets the better of it.)

BLAT'S TALES

HOW BLAT'S NAME WAS AVENGED UPON THE TAKER OF ASSO-CIATIVE LIBERTIES WITH IT

"Does your name signify 'blot', or 'bladder'?" Blat was asked. "It doesn't dignify, so why should it signify?" came his verbally evasive non-reply.

"Then, in short, it's a misnomer for 'blah'?" his questioner taunted. Blat angrified. He took his tormentor by the shoulder blades, and shook his clavicles loose, letting the other bones start their cascading log-rolling at their weak-sister link in the whole broken-up daisy-chain. Wherewith, Blat stuck in a verbal laceration as well: "My name here breaks your bony sticks and marrow-stones," mangled Blat in furious emphasis. His antagonist quietly withered.

Posthumously, the latter declared, "Blat, you've made me skin my words alive, and eat them down my rotting throat, while you gloat and survive."

To which Blat's rejoinder took a rhyme form:

"You took up my name in vain.
Just lie there, where you're lain.
You've taken your word back; but are slain.
Your name slandering was taken up in vain.
Now it's shoved back on you, in disdain:
put deep down inside your loss, and on my gain."

No reply came from the penalized offender. Blat's name was the same as before. But now it stood inviolable, for defense had made it heroic. It was a deadly name: one mocker had proved it. Blat himself needn't die for it. Let it be injured, and his revenge would exceed the nominal, just as a man stands out ahead of what he's called by, and abstract honor must be settled by his bones' integrity.

That's how Blat stands to attention, when his name is wafted aloft.

BLAT AS THE DISCIPLE, APOSTLE, AND BREAKNECK SPEND-THRIFT OF AN UNFORESEEN, UNPROPHESIED, SPONTA-NEOUSLY OUTBURSTING FUTURE. FOR HE'S LADEN WITH NO MEMORY, AND LIMPS ALONG WITHOUT A PAST. HIS EXPERI-ENCE ISN'T RECORDED, AND IS ALWAYS BEING REPLACED. SO HE BLUNDERS INTO, BUT DOESN'T LEARN FROM, AND NEVER USES. HE PLUNGES AHEAD, ARTLESS, PURE, PRO-TECTED BY HIS VERY UNPREPAREDNESS. COLLIDING WITH THE FUTURE, HE TREATS IT LIKE A BURST BUBBLE, AND GOES ON. IT DOESN'T SERVE TO REPLENISH HIS STOCK, FOR HE PUTS NOTHING BEHIND HIM. HE BLUNDERS OUT ON OPEN HEADLONG FREEDOM. YET BLAT SURVIVES, THOUGH NOT BY HIS MANAGING. HIS VERY VULNERABILITY EXPOSES HIM TO THE RIGHT CHANCE, ON OCCASION. AND SO FAR HE'S LIV-ING AHEAD, HAVING LEARNED NO HABIT TO FORTIFY ANY CAUTION. AN EXPERIENCE, SWEEPS RIGHT BY HIM, IN AND OUT, BEING LOST ON CONTACT. THERE'S MORE IN FRONT. HE DOESN'T HOARD, NOTHING TO FALL BACK ON. THERE'S IM-MEDIATE SPENDING, AT ALL TIMES. HE CAN'T SAVE, SO THE SQUANDERING IS HIS LIVING, AND NOTHING ON HAPPENING EVER REACHES WISDOM'S STORE. HIS MOTION OPENS INTO EVER AGING INNOCENCE. HE HASN'T RUN OUT OF TIME; SO HE RUNS INTO IT, CONTINUOUSLY: MEETING HIS DWINDLING FUTURE AT ANY INEXPERIENCED TURN. BLAT IS AN IMPETU-OUS FORGETFULNESS. UNDENTED, HE HAS NO RECOURSE TO SUFFERING, FOR THE MOMENT IS SOON OVER. BEING IN-STANTANEOUSLY HURT, HE RETAINS NO SAVOR OF IT. HIS MOMENTUM IS BEING GATHERED, WITH NO TAIL.

When Blat was finally asked, "Who were your antecedents?," he said that being a man of the future how could he have had any? With that retort, he prevailed, due to its surprise. His open future draws upon his past obscurity, feeling free from having to make reference to the lurking traditionalism potent by precedence. Even with turning older, his past is all that more a blur, keeping his future a virgin to be ravished by a bold pioneerdom. With no trail to follow, he innovates the same errors, heaping fresh and innocent vigor on his stale and repetitive blunders. Experience can't teach him, so he can't get his bearings by learning from it. He starts out new and vulnerable, with the world open before him: no compass, chart, or map to steer by, for all his having lived close to fifty years. Which way to turn? Any, or none. With no wisdom, he has no, or all, choices.

"I invent as I go along. My discoveries are original, for I have no memory. Whatever happened to me, or befell me, is as though such an event had never occurred. I'm bound by no habit. What's to be is not historically prepared for, within my lifetime, for I have no pattern of archetypes to deduce predictability or likelihood from, or take an average on possibility's range. To be so unprepared is to be brave at peril. This puts my ignorance in a boasting position. I've compiled no ready chronicle to refer to as proof against foolhardiness in the days to be. The same fish who was hooked up by bait before and then tossed back, will return and go for the same evil hook, heaping a fresh coat of blood on his barely congealed previous coat. That fish is a sucker. *I* swim in blind waters against unforeseen obstacles. My future is an openly exposed wound for the world to take pot shots at. My not learning from the past is like a Christian Scientist resorting to no doctor when a sick emergency comes up. Instead of the past fortifying me, I go naked, into the new. My security is perched on whatever's chronically precarious. My stumbling is almost assured."

That's Blat's testament. Isn't he the masochist? He's a prey to the malice of fortune's indifference. His bad luck has been established as determined, for he can't avert it. He doesn't *woo* disaster; but he doesn't go out of his way to avoid it: it comes unrecognized, and rams him right through. What accounts for his having survived all these years? The future is touched by his blind faith in it, the trust he generously reposes in its reputedly fickle store. So it's cast him under its protection. He's a fond pet of it.

The helpless are very disarming. That's Blat's trick. His innocence is a weapon, to advantage. As it's his only one, it's of course genuine. Blat is a rare one. He's almost fifty years old, but half a century has guided him only by the chaotic rules of oblivion. So with him it's onward, for even mentally there's nothing behind him. Those fifty years have gone the way of dust from a sure matron's broom. Blat's clean slate is eager and forward. When he's slammed down, he soon doesn't know it. No wounds to lick, or heal with rankle. Pain has been eased of his sharp memory.

Suffering sloughed aside into oblivion. That's the key to Blat's resilience. All harm becomes unconsciously past: so what harm can it do him? He's free to falter on error, and recover from any slip. If method or doctrine were given to fearlessness, that's it. The careless optimistic approach, based on nothing save the futility of nursing pessimism.

Blat on the future: "So it's to be. When that happens, must I hoard it? There'll still be more allotted. And when *that* gives out, I'm done for. Death is when no future is left, for immediate consumption. Its stock has all been squandered, without precisely having been accounted for. Even now, with years remaining, the future is all I own. I depend on it, even for my nostalgia, and for being retrospective. When my allowance gives out—"

He didn't complete that. *What* didn't he complete? Completion itself: the finality and nature of an end, once life is removed, past or no past. Youth is rich with an unspent future. Age declines into poverty, and turns penniless. But with the final declaration of bankruptcy, there's no solvency even for begging. So Blat believes in what's to be. And his belief is narrowing.

THE PAST UNBLATTED

Blat wasn't always this way. But before he was, he couldn't have been Blat, either.

HOW TO OVERTHROW FATE

"How do you pronounce 'failure'?" the infant Blat asked his nursery teacher. "Failure will be pronounced on you, in due time," she forecast. This was Blat's preparatory education. His life solidly lived up to it, as the forewarning was made prophetic in the process of experience taking its destined course.

He graduated from school and assumed his failure role outside in the real world of life. By mingling in a crowd, he chanced to come upon his ex nursery teacher, who instantly recognized him as though many years had been a mere glass. "I always knew it, I could feel it in your bones, that failure that you were to be. And you haven't failed me," she gratefully intoned, caressing his hand, acknowledging his exemplariness as the docile model of a true passive student. "By your name— Blat—it was possible to construct its synonymship with the otherwise disembodied concept of 'failure', Now 'failure' has you for a person, and you have something to be, definite, to be identified by, or defined into. To believe in fate gives a shape to the world. You were being formed, and I had a hand in it. I allied myself with the inevitable, and you proved malleably educable, when your formativeness was just starting to grow. You fit into what you were stamped by, and the extension of the premise confirmed a logical conclusion, You've been a very edifying and instructive example of the limitations and possibilities of achievement. You directly *became* something: a feat that others are dilatory about. As an educator, I'm warmheartedly vindicated, by your superbly simple case. Your solution came before there was even a problem. Harmony *can* be made out of chaos; the secret is to be firm. Your failure has a universal law about it. Its opposite, success, is contained in it somewhat.

"When I got a hold of you, you were an earlier Blat. You're still the later product. Unity and form have molded time to their design. I can die in that happy knowledge. Your manifest failure realized the potential I could detect in you. More amorphous students are too plastic to pin down. They won't hold still for destiny to assign a specific to them. You were from the first suited to your developed failure. You wear it becomingly, it's your fitting emblem to be. Your infantile record card had the name of Blat on it. Then all that was required was to insist upon my intelligent foresight. Our commitment to your failure launched it out on a steady tide. It has come home, made and assured. Your name of 'Blat' is connected through association with what I ascribed to it. The teacher has her reward. The taught have not been refractory. I made some sense on an emergent life. It's matured, like an epithet. My teacher's career is what you've become, You're my life's work of all the art and science I ever had. Now I'm old, Blat. I'll die soon. You won't betray me after that, will you?"

Blat looked down at his old nursery teacher. "I'm a *successful* failure," he stressed. "That split of opposites is like an atomic split: potentially explosive. My failure will ripen. You'll be gone. And my failure will convert itself. 'Blat' will have successful overtones."

This morbidified the teacher. She scurried away.

Blat was left with free will, the fatal curse removed, no more tyrant of a destiny. "I'll plainly succeed," he wooed, wooing his pregnant Future of himself. She still stood coyly away. She revealed nothing, sphinx-like. He would have to pursue her more actively. Then she'd yield their union's child, the child of former Blat and his wedded Future to be. As yet, Blat was only an embryonic duplicate of the established family Blat, which would be settled down to actual existence once that nursering teacher witch of Blat's helpless childhood would oblige the cause of freedom by espousing Death for herself. Liberated, Blat and his future Future would wed for Success'es legitimacy, their bouncing and expectant offspring. That would be a dear reversal to Blat's steady doom at the hands of an imposed Fate, The defeat of Failure would give rise to the right release. And Blat, unknown from before, would step into a new birthright.

THE LAW OF EATING; ESPECIALLY AS CARRIED INTO EXECUTION BY BLAT'S AVERAGE EXAMPLE

When the meal was set down in front of the particularly hungry Blat (with a clank and slither of the crockeryware against the resounding tabletop made of shock-absorbent wood pores surrounded in each case by the wood itself of leatherlike corkiness) there was bound to be a reaction. The first course was demolished by Blat. He was just as coarse for the second one. The food began being eaten one after another, going the way of all food when famished opportunity meets with edible commodity. Blat bolted, gorged, and choked, with equal facility, and the mouth was ravenous with teeth. And the filling stomach spread out and out. Blat privately expanded into the universe, There was more to Blat than before, and his self-possession took on a corporeal girth. He had more lattitude, and far more Blattitude. And a stouter attitude.

The meal was in a state of flattertude, The relative position of Blat was one of fattertude. He was stuffed in dense layers of mattertude. The physical idea of eating was now redundant with plattertude.

So Blat went to sleep, and slept softly. Hark, even now, he's in his sleep. He's peaceful. His dinner is eaten. And *he* makes a meal, for sweet oblivion. Blat is being dined on. And when he's thoroughly consumed, he'll have a waking. And he'll be devoured by his rhythmically periodical appetite. Devoutly sacrificed, the devoured devourer. The stout stand of Blat, to hold on to life's state till he's counted out. Not till then will he let go. There are meals to be counted up. Which one will permanently still the recurrence of appetite? Can one eating put the cycle to a solved end? His experiments grow grosser. To find a meal that doesn't *lend* fullness, but keeps fullness full always. To stoke so heroically proportioned a goal, his nobly-portioned eating increases fullfold, the fool making bold to light on that classic meal that's everlasting, or be weighted at last, waited on in perpetual fasting, in *being* some outer vastness'es lasting meal, ending Blat as a mortal dish. The eating fish is eaten in turn, then the larger eater is eaten by an even larger. While Blat wolfs it down, God, eating last, waits for having the whole of Blat to gnaw a larger hole than that whole into, to assimilate digestive Blat into a law of dietary abstaining. The eater's sleep and the eaten's sleep are two unrelated kinds. Better to leave them apart than to speculate on some common secret link between them.

Blat alternates his tiredness with the chewing up of former life. He's in one of his pre-former life days. He's on the consuming side; *being* consumed will operate from the anaesthetic of that opposite side, so deeply propped on indefinite postponement. Blat is a one-way-working appetite, through which his life functions. This alone is appropriate to his care. He serves the self until a radical reversal overrules his expansive indulgence and topples a lifetime in the products of pleasure, measured in the private chamber of the stomach's tides and fortunes spanned to the full elastic allotment of fluctuations and groans. The relief of emptiness, and the time it takes. The inner Blot, unsocial in a vat of solitude, the stirred, unsettled kettle containing sustenance momentary but porous with its obsolescing turnovers and replenishment-hunger. The churning industrial interior self-contained and self-sustaining, at selfish odds in common with all men outside. Blat's assumed universal, by his properties and paraphernalia, all the equipage and propensities standard in man's slavish eating, habitually individual, but invariably collective. One eating Blat, or the Blatkind of everyone.

BLAT IN HISTORY: HIS RECORD AS A PUBLIC FIGURE. (INTEL-LECTUAL VIGOR SAPPED BY INFLUENTIAL POWER: THE NUL-LIFICATION OF INDIVIDUAL IDEAS, TO BALANCE SOCIAL IN-TERESTS AND PROMOTE POLITICAL HARMONY IN THE ARTI-FICIAL UNION OF MEN. BUT WHEN DID BLAT EVER HAVE HIS OWN IDEAS? EVEN WHEN AN UNKNOWN, IN PRIVATE LIFE.)

Blat's opinion was sought in all matters. He was crowded around by opinion seekers. "But I'm not decided, just as of yet," he admitted, when pressed to commit his answers onto public media like television, radio, newspapers, and magazines. The microphones were thrust to his closed mouth, by importunous propagators or transmitters of thrilling, live public documents, for popular consumption. "Stop querying me," he begged, but the insistent quizzing got more vehement. How to account for the widespread curiosity? Why would many people care just what Blat thought? The more he wondered, the more futile of explanation it all seemed, and the strangeness of it all over-came him, the inexplicable estranged him from his wondering source. Now here he was, inundated with snap queries. The less he answered, the more the bombardment continued. He was at a loss. He was helplessly in demand.

And Blat was overwhelmed. His belief was sought out, on every conceivable matter.

"I haven't decided, I'm not sure," he frankly replied, armed only with uncertainty. That didn't stop his assaulters. They lashed at him, like detectives tracking a murderer. The pub-lic wanted to know; these responsible agents of the public were determined to extract the lowdown from recalcitrant Blat. He squirmed on all their hooks, and wasn't let off. He was trapped in the center of fact-finding. They bore down on him, with their numerical weight.

Glibly, he gave out *any* answer. To decrease the tension; the pressure. Or to let off his vent, unpent. And not be kept under constraint.

All over the broad land, at that moment, in the press, periodicals, on television, over radio, Blat's voice was heard commonly, or the words of it read. The interest was widespread. Blat's non-message prevailed, in central communication. All minds were filled with what he was saying. The news went round in a streak. I

How to reduce crime?

Blat: "By striking at its root. And ruthlessly eradicating it."

The danger of overpopulation, with not enough food to go around, what solution would you recommend?

"At the present time, nothing drastic or headstrong should rash desperation dash into. In time, the problem will afford its own answer, or excessive war will carve the question out and only suggest another."

The merging of the sexes, often indistinguishable from each other in the radical appearance of the younger generation. How should this be offset?—or should it be left alone?

"The tendency is not too alarming. Appearances to the contrary, underneath it all is the same old act of lust as usual, once the hair is let down and the clothes removed. Nature has always been conservative, in so vital an issue, and is bound to remain so, under any administration that our lifetimes may see rise or decline, upholding a neutral stability of a nonpolitical nature."

What challenging events must be taken care of at once, otherwise the world would be not far from danger?

"There should be more investigation. What's the rush? We can rely on astronomy: it takes time."

How can politics be improved, to ensure more representative governments that give more people what they need and take away less?

"This is so essential, it must be thoroughly gone into. It's of international importance."

Thus Blat aired his opinions. Cautiously, deliberately, knowing they would be listened to and in many cases believed. People are so credulous, care must be taken of what's mentally fed at them. Blat was now a world citizen, in general, but in particular he had his country's welfare at heart. He must choose his words in accordance with his most considered ideas. He had been forced into responsibility. Let him courageously acquit himself of it. Nation-wide elections were coming up. He was sure to be nominated, on the strength of his current limelight. He was now a known figure, and respected throughout. He mustn't let down the majority. His power to disappoint must never be used. Nor should he lead the political body astray. Blat was prominent. How did he get to be?

Blat doesn't know, nor does anyone else. But there he is. Blat, potentially a statesman. Suddenly the dominant candidate.

Blat is no longer a private individual. He used to have personal opinions. But now, every thought he thinks goes through the enlarger into cosmopolitan magnitude, exerting vast, even if unintentional, influence, His ideas count, so magnified heroically, outside his control utterly. He hardly dares think otherwise, than in the maximum social coverage. He's consensus-opinionated, with his huge, diversified amalglomeration of a public following, all literally strangers to the formerly private Blat before recruited into a mass-focalized personage of noble open dignity obedient to the obedience of his sacred employer, the Many, to whom he's their renowned slave highly appointed.

He once had a freedom of ideas, in his personal irresponsibility.

Now, his eminence is such, that his mental freedom has stiffened rigid with so many interbalancing regards.

Frankly, Blat is scared. He doesn't know *what* to think.

What a position to be in! And the consequences, how dread. He's in awe up to the hilt, of his very self. The pressure is relent-

less, besides having a murderous weight. The luxury of innocence is ill-afforded. Blat is in for it. The people look to him.

He wins a sweeping election by a landslide majority. He's
dumped hard, into the loftiest of offices. Any word he cares
to commit, in his official role, has devastating impact. Speech
is paralyzed with pulsating alarm, it's on the spot, the sounds
weigh, they're recorded. Blat is afraid to be extreme, he should
seek refuge in the solid percentage of a middle position, to
balance all possibilities suddenly grown political. He must es-
pouse some compromising "mean," and not branch too far out.
Wild disaster treads in wait outside each moderate boundary.
Blat must exert care, to an agonizing delicacy. Or else! The most
terrifically persistent pressure. He can't let the people down.
Let him be prudent. His principles are bound to moderation.
He must weigh everything.

(The one with the weight on him is the one who weighs.
This is the natural and moral law of human power.)

Blat is really in for it. He must watch out.

One wrong move—and catastrophe, with his endorsement,
would be let loose.

Take care. On guard.

Blat. He censors every thought. He seals himself in a vacuum. Dreadful extremes converge precariously. He must ward
them off! With all political expedience.

Blat has lost the faculty of thought, under the pressing demands of his public dehumanized office.

His role is the tyrant of a watchdog over him. He's airlessly
guarded. Daringness is out. Each breath might be decisive,

The small price to pay, for his undying fame.

He's too immortal to take a stand. *All* stands are *equally*
his. Blat understands. He shrinks, he's meek. Every breath is
cautious. So much depends. The world is crushing him down,
issues and events are now momentous. The statesman has
emerged. The individual has been choked out. There *is* no Blat.

While his fame increases.

And he's denounced, as well. The growth of his rivals. Many of them, with him their target. He's earned all his enemies. The world has well noted him.

The endlessness of Blat. He can't perish. The publicity on him is now a record of history. He's the historical personage, of this trying age.

Blat. Reduced, expanded, into the enormity of a public self. He's shrunk into greatness. But his enemies are gaining.

He's displaced. Ousted from office. Fallen.

The former statesman. The world and years go by. His official capacity is past. He'd like to regain his private choice of ideas. His opinions had once been solicited; by popular acclaim. But even then, there had been no opinions. Was that the factor of his public rise?

What *is* thought? The re-individualized Blat is researching this. He's after an independent mental life. For his own private use.

The collective group-world is going on. Without benefit, or detraction, of Blat. History has others to make use of. More foils to be collected, on route.

Society, minus Blat. To whose loss?

Blat sits quiet, and reads a book. A non-influential activity. It's not a wielding of power. It's a private concern. The book unleashes thinking. Blat is evoked to untapped opinions, their latency restored. What's his view? The commentators from television are ready, and radio hawks, reporters and feature journalists, columnists. For the outside projection, in public channels of communication, of the interior Blat, the mind at work. Ideas relative to any subject. One man, at thought. The world would heed in, and hook him up. An accumulation of interest has now surrounded Blat, preparing the convenience of his comeback. But the mounting pressure decreases his mental force. He's turning feeble, in the head: so much to accommodate.

BLAT'S MOST ULTIMATE PLAN FOR POSTHUMOUS REVENGE FOR THE DISGRACE OF BEING HUMILIATED BY GIRLS' REJECTING HIM BECAUSE HIS BODY COULD SUSTAIN LUST ONLY IN IMPOTENCE

When two girls *both* wanted to reject Blat, Blat was in a dilemma to choose between them. His choice would go to the rejection that offered the least humiliation. Finally, when the time grew near to decide, he got himself rejected by the prettier of the two. The uglier was so offended by this indirect insult, that *she* rejected him as well. That *really* hurt him. Blat would never throw his fifty years at a girl again. It would be thrown right back at him, twice as viciously, and disgrace him with one hundred years. How could he live it down? But prior to that, how had he expected to live it up? Only his personal death would sign its terminus on those silly, pseudo-romantic bickerings he so detested when girls enticed him to grow foolish. If he couldn't outgrow the folly. He'd in-decay it, thanks to death's instinctive restraint. Inertia would calm him down, and weed out his stinking lust. The sedative pill would still his alarming anxiety about the enormous progress his impotence was making, in undermining his manly sturdiness. The increasingly inferior virility of his inner manhood would have less secret-pent, more public vent, once, by official stroke, his death became solemnly notarized. Then Blat and women would be severed. His soul would fly one way, and their bodies sink another. He exulted at the outwitting of them. Their carnal survival would be fitting, to match and mate Blat's contrary ascendancy to the bodiless glory he knew would deliver him from shame at not being able to perform sin's rigorous act. Vengeance would be sublime: it failed on the *other* key.

THE UNCRITICAL BLAT AS A MUSICAL ENTHUSIAST

"The robust vulgarity of say a big pompous popular opera by the buffo Verdi," said Blat with more melodic gusto than musical discernment, exposing his voluptuary instincts, "I prefer to the bland, colorless, insipid, tepid, dilute, vapid, and indifferent good taste of something too sterile to be tainted with the smackèd blessing of vulgar, boisterous heartiness."

His antagonist launched a wry "Why?" Blat swayed into defense of his position, by elaborating this straightforward explanation:

"I don't like sophistication, when it leads to sterility. The beating heart may be cosmopolitanized out of it. What's left might be nice art; but 'So what!?' must be shouted to it." That's what Blat said, but the critics didn't agree. Why should they?—it would ruin their livelihood.

So Blat listened to a blaringly loud, sentimentally unashamed, overly overt, garish, unabashed, and non-delicate work of delight, It gave him joy. He depended for a livelihood on a noncritical occupation. So he heard happily, and was freely able to appreciate like a mindless but pleased child. He needn't conform to the day's lofty standards of intelligently cold, withdrawn, and negative appraisal. When the music bombarded him, there was no guilt to interrupt it. So it roared in, with full exuberance. It took him by his nerves, and gave him a good dosing over, He wouldn't recover. It centered direct to memory, and the thrill was always shaking. The composer awarded him a citation for delicious use of what the composer delivered to birth while still on this thumping side of pre-angelic earth, when loins and heart and brains were in their blasting unison transported to sound as sense would have it, when sense was open to every shock, with the withstanding appetite in the voluminous echo chamber. A bombastic triumph between strangers, passing through death.

THOUGH DEFICIENT IN SYMPTOMS, BLAT SUCCESSFULLY FAKES HYPOCHONDRIA

I

Blat realized that essentially nothing was wrong with him—bar of course the literal metaphysical "everything". So he started to imagine that he had imaginary ailments from the imaginary point of view. Since Blat was six feet two with weight proportionate his figure, it looked as though death's door, far from ever opening for him, was locked and jammed from the inside with reinforced concrete and would always be stuck. That's how robust his health radiated, to keep mortality at bay.

Since he had good health, he had so much to lose—he had so much from which it was possible for something to go wrong. This decided him on a course of hypochondria. But now that he had become a hypochondriac (sworn in on the spot, self-pledged, taking the vow to complain all the more for the fewer symptoms, to compensate with mind over matter for being hearty, hale, and wholesome in the body, requiring a poisoned mind to stem the tide of physically good health), he realized that what his hypochondria desperately needed was a cure. His worry was now in earnest, and genuine misgivings gave way to acute anxiety, which altered his heart beat and his metabolic rate. His whole body (or what was left of it) crumbled in a heap, afflicted with the dread, rampaging plague of his hypochondria, a self-perpetuating disease to which even the victim was contagious, since *having* it was no guarantee against immunity, and the dose was too large (out of hand already, and galloping away) for the harmless precautionary of inoculation. His only hope was to see a doctor. It was his last chance.

He was seated in the doctor's office, having secured an emergency (or emerge in an imaginarily emergency) appointment, even outside of the stern physician's visiting hours. On the nurse's record sheet he gave his name as Blat, which was his nominal way of telling the truth. But who was he, outside of a name? His hypochondria had included amnesia, in its consumptive imperialism that took gradual dominion over all the provinces of himself as annexed and conquered territory, colonializing. Therefore Blat had added a severe identity problem, at the heart of his ego's void, to his real bodily infirmities that he so vividly had subjected to the corrosive decadence of his highly destructive imagination. On that path, further down, if persisted in, lay insane neurosis. Thus real danger came from indulging the once-thought-harmless faculty, the imagination.

"Why are you here?" the doctor probed. "To insult you—I mean consult you." Blat corrected himself. His slips of the tongue gave Freudian evidence against having a simple illness which could be simply treated. "You're quite a case," the doctor concluded after billing the patient and easing him to the door. "But you haven't cured me yet," was Blat's legitimate complaint, feeling short-changed and unfairly dealt with by the doctor's off-hand and cursory manner, and summarily being dismissed. "Where are your prescriptions?" asked Blat but the door was already shut adding the shock of psychosis to an indignant but mounting list of hypochondriacal ailments that plagued the sufferer. It was costly, his money was running out. He would have to become a charity case, unless what was wrong could be radically checked, promptly purged, wrenched out, and firmly eradicated. This was unlikely, since nature took time to heal, in recovery's low trudge uphill against the plunging hordes of distress. Blat felt wretched. What should he do?

Only one recourse lay open to him: go to another doctor. Despite his dwindling purse and depleting bank reserves, it was the only drastic step to make, under the iron dictation of extreme circumstance and the grave prompting of duress.

II

He was quite a wreck as he entered the next doctor's office. What was left of his health was all in the past, and even that, on retrospect, paraded under a banner of dubious credentials. He could hardly be considered to be himself. But define the self.

The doctor looked fat and jolly. Accordingly, Blat felt optimistic. "What's wrong?' he was asked, in such a tone as though it was silly to be upset. All Blat could do was grin, while the fat doctor led him under a gross beam, with a bland positive approach. "Then why are you taking my time and making me take your money?" asked the good-natured doctor, which struck Blat to such hilarity that despite himself he matched the good doctor's mirth with quite a healthy laugh. His bile was being purged, the while his vile humors were beguiled down the drain. Genial flows secreted rosy glows, while his restored faculties took an intoxicant of natural energy from a grand discharge of pure glands that purred contented tones from organic beatitude. Blat was suffused in the high happy plenitude of health's subdued ecstasy. Burdened thus, his hypochondria was put under a cloud, and condemned to its transparent falsity. He couldn't go through with his ruse, and health began to assert its truth, released from its bonds of deception that imposed a slick veneer of sick pall on a fundamental constitution of impeccable functioning. What a bare-faced liar he had been! He must atone and make it good, in front of his benevolent doctor whose stomach protruded good will and amiable prospects. Blat had been a fool in disguise, now to doff the false suit. He'd cling to his pretense, and watch it subside.

"Doctor," he began, "I'm a hypochondriac—how can I cure it?"

"Don't worry about it: the doctor replied, and forced a clean bill of health upon Blath whose vigor could brazen no more its deceptive negation. Hearty force bellowed in him, like the sun drenching the heavens with the torrid exhalation of its periodically unshackled ardor, pouring summer loose from a captivity in frozen mothballs, and reversing the harsh reign of ill-tempered winter that had subjugated nature to its bitter-blown spell that perversely kept downtrodden every robust specimen of animation created to a term of life.

Blat paid the doctor on the spot, abjuring the bill, and strode out cured of his brief bout with the mental exercise of his hypochondria. It had cost him some dollars, but the relief was so satisfying that soon he'd incur the disease again, to reproduce the cycle and repeat the pleasant reassurance of so splendid an outcome. His cure had addicted him.

BLAT'S SELF-DISPARAGING INSIGNIFICANCE, FOR NOT HAVING RADICALLY EXTENDED EVOLUTION

The human race had been given a shove into prominence by the laborious process of evolution long before Blat ever entered the stage. So when he came on, the stage was raised, and he had a platform to stand on. This pre-stature helped him to be able to reach for the heights. The heights were not daunted. They kept themselves out of reach, refusing to condescend to a mere recent climber. So Blat had to be content. He had never looked a star in the face, only to have it blink him down. That's why Blat never goes down to pray before the altar of evolution. The lowly amoeba knew its humble place. But Blat's grandeur has always deluded him, for he's never attained it. "Why have I a face, only to lose it?" he angrily declares. "My rank lost caste ever since the early days of my nonentity stripped my vanity of glorious ego and took the air out of my name. I've been downgraded, before I had a chance to even have a grade. My birth showed me the way out into loss. Honor's been spurious, with no decency to uphold. Should I be grateful for evolution? It started man, but who am I to complete him, being only another example not far removed from man as he's always essentially been. My quantity is added to the species, like superredundant proof. That's all my addition has been. Virtually a minus, for all that man has been the same, no thanks to whether I've either existed or not. Man goes on, so why should I? How much less than negligible has my contribution ever contributed! All I am is for me. The race could do without me, I'm its unvital part. I'm substantial as Blat. Mankind is substantial just as it is, without my extra shadow to trail it in these modern times. My me lacks significance. It's only important for the self, on that one individual scale. Outside, where is it?

THE PLOT TO RIP APART POOR BLAT AND HIS DEEPLY ATTACHED NOSTALGIA

When Blat feels nostalgia coming over him, he evacuates his timeless soul from the present moment of wherever or whatever, discarding anything not evocative of the nostalgia he's summoned by. He does hold on to what, however immediate, gives substantive contribution, in contrast or harmony, to his nostalgia's prevailing fancy and levitating whimsy or weighty poignancy, selecting from the current instant a charging fuel to stoke its need.

Has Blat so orderly a control over his inner life?

No, it's a clumsy mess, awkward and uncouth. He's a driveling slave to the past. He's sticky, and clings to it.

By what particulars is he glued to nostalgia?

Girls and places and times. Scenes, events, activities. Past phases of his life. Friends no more seen, customs no more indulged. Whatever retrospect forms a fondness for, he's hooked to. Whatever he used to enjoy (without knowing it then, or shrugging it dismissingly) but now can't bring back or repeat in act and use. Passive memory frets, and he longs to do it again. He pines for *her*, or yearns for *that*. Nostalgia is his vast mental substitute for all those gone things that miss the repetition of replacement. It mimics those diverse ghosts, in phantom hallucination. Poor, poor Blat. He had so much that's lost now. Former gratifications return to haunt. He's bound to them, by sentiment's time-honored loyalty. Sentimentality, for recollecting out of proportion with the collection's meager application today: a value for outdated usefulness, distorting time's balance in lopsided favor of an unpracticable past. Blat regrets he can't haul it back in again, like a tangible object entirely renovated.

Blat is fussing in his brain, for dead things of private significance. Nostalgia is a solitary affair, lonely with grief.

Of all he's bereft of?

Alas!, for the pale and vanished fondnesses of the earlier Blat, that the later Blat is a fool for. His sobbing adoration for the unreclaimable. Blat now can't be and have what he was and had. Is that only pathetic, or does it loom into larger tragedy?

Only a philosopher can answer that, with sufficient vagueness at his disposal. What Blat needs is to go to a philosopher for periodic injections of theorum, abstracts, generalium, formulates, and pessimectum. His remedies will be cured of therapy, by temporal applications, and the purge will lift him from rear assaults. He needs to wind his clock ahead, to be relieved of a backheavy weight. It's in his interest to tell him so, so he won't mope, and droop under his melancholy burden, Let him speculate on a friendly future, and lean toward its inclination. Or resurge what's current with present interest, in waves of fascination and enthusiasm, to realert his forward faculties. Let rejuvenation act by today, to stave off an inferior remembrance of a better yesterday. Tell Blat all that. Do you have his special ear?

No, the other one.

Well, pour it in, anyhow. It'll get mixed up; inside.

And Blat will be repaired?

His nostalgia condemned to half.

Fifty years reinforce his nostalgia.

So much dead weight. Pare him of it, at once.

He'll be geared for action?

And make heady room of Now. Impetuate a living deed, not an ancient thought. Initiate unsentimental behavior, by reality's altered law. Direct him to the changes, and force him to reluctantly accept them, despite the lure of previous years. Harden him to altered fact, and unsoften him from those futile musings. Cut off Blat before, isolate the present version, and unlink them. Nostalgia thrives by time's unity. Slice it, then. And let the divided worm wriggle in separate paths.

Blat would detest your sternness.

So would sternness detest Blat, till he proves his mettle by *its* standards. Rigor Blat off the cosiness he left behind, adapt him to a harsh mode of forgetting. Nostalgia is weakening, enervating. Vigor lives off real nourishment, not once-fare. Push him into the startlingness of Today.

He'll dwell at the immediate, however unpleasant its sensation compared with a selected bouquet of grand yesterdays. We'll reduce him to present impoverishment, and strip his heart. Blat will have to choke on dirt; the scented echo of a former dust, however it does suffice him, will be his deprivation. Blat will move on: forsake the glorious, and accept the real.

Are we doing him a favor?

It's for his own good.

We'll enforce this strict virtue. An austere diet off the actual; not those creamy dinings on protracted luxuriance. We'll surgicate his brain.

We'll redeem him. No more empty dreams, for him.

Blat will get a tearing down.

And be renovated down to an earthy base on a true site. We'll place him in the present time.

About time. We'll edify his edifice, and instruct his structure, and enlighten his delight, and illuminate his ruminate.

But will it be Blat?

Not as known. He'll be our invention, not the creature he had created in himself.

Have we constructed?; or have we *destructed?*

Divide Blat from his nostalgia; *then* tend the result. Let our zeal be for the act; unless *he* converts *us*.

Assuming we've changed him; I already have nostalgia for the Blat that was.

So endearing. So past-thronged. We were monsters to interfere. We violated his soul's most sacred archives.

What an undoing! Let's undo the undoing!

Good: by not doing it.

BLAT TAKING THE CONCRETE BY ITS EMPIRICAL

Blat had to have a thing before he could think. He couldn't form his thought along nothingness'es indistinct line.

WHERE DOES BLAT FIT IN?: LONG AGO, OR IN THE FUTURE? NEITHER. HIS PRESENT PLACE IS NOW. OTHERWISE WATCH HIM EVAPORATE.

(A Dissertation (In Miniature) of How Blat is Most Blat When Immediate, But Pales off into Insignificance in the Dim Past, or in the Equally Insubstantial Future, Both Vague, Abstract, UnBlatian, the More Removed from the Instantaneity of the Only Durable Time for Blat, Otherwise the Flat Earth Falls off when Duration Ends, for Failing Blat to be the Lonely Companion of Chaos, in Speculative Yonder, in the Metaphysical Vast, Either Direction. Past History or the As-Yet-to-Be.

Find Blat Here, at Once. He Has Everywhere Else to be Lost in, and All the Time in the World that doesn't Condense into Now. Blat's a Haystack, Seen through a Needle's Solitary Eye; But then the Farm Changes its Location. Will the Haystack Remain? Or did Your Lose the Blat—Finding Needle? Or are YOU Lost, s well?: Which would increase the Difficulty of Pinning Blat Down and Uncovering His Huge Whereabouts in Time's Prolonged Desert or Abandoned Farm Country or Desolate Stretches of Temporal Suburbia, the Slums of any Moment but Now. Once there's Blat, He's Achieved, or He's not, Depending on what You do. If You're there at the Time, to do it.)

Blat looked for his lost opportunity. It had been lost and never been replaced such a few years ago that Blat couldn't recall it having been lost. But how was it his to have lost it? He followed an infallible direction into the past leading recessively into the retro and rear where a few nostalgia-laden echoes surrendered their dewy spectres to the dusty backwards sweep of the intangibility-stirring broom. It set up a vibration of windy trembles, a series of waves scurrying to evoke. No memory image was offered up: just some dull, remote remorse. From no definite cause. It wasn't enough. Was there an opportunity not taken? Only vagueness could work back. What could this settle, or establish, or hint at with drifting pointers, using no material to leave a trace? The turning was mental. Where look, among ideas? By "opportunity," what? And how was "lost" determined? So Blat gave up, and came back forward. The current present was a brisker bracing. Blat felt better giving the past his back, so that his front came more approachably into view. To expose some later opportunities, better dealt with than those whose loss was shaded inexactly outside actual grip, faded somewhere behind, too nebulous to come up and be converted into vitality's usages, employing a new set of modes to work toward something, something just as vague, hidden behind veils of future. *Way* out in front there was an equal dimness to the far out back. Blat could only catch the light between them: while the light was still there.

Just at that bend of the curve, where Blat could *be*. That's the holding-still moment, with violent motions on either side, and paler wastelands diverging into opposite infinities, both cut off from the reserves of fortifying sense, the supply lines whose provisions can be hauled into use to try the current purpose to prove a nourished need. Blat would stick close to his supply lines. Astray could mean starvation, or the mental infirmity of insignificance. Life plays compact to be sturdy: when far-ranging, it gets lost in dangled obscurity, stretching the hinges loose, and unworking the core's robust strength for the surrounding structure. "Don't trust the vast past, or the far future:" That became the narrowed motto of contracted Blat. The nearer to him, the more vigorous was time's intense color. Let the rest go to waste. Utilize what's close. What's far afield loses its "whatness," becomes a guessing theory of dubious solidity and only alleged substance. It would take a *wizard* to exploit *that*. Or a special mystic who thrives on not exploiting things for the practical increase of gain, selfishly considered. Blat wasn't of that calibre. So he's a Now man.

And his picture is vivid. Now swings things into focus. A clarity that speaks for itself. Blat needn't resort to uncanny interpretation. A strength of reality, in the compression of time into this pulse, feel it here, leave that beat alone, or let that one come to be when it looms too far off, and drop the other one behind you, time must be squandered, the waste and drain of all but what the moment selects, as its own, temporarily. That's Blat's immediate attitude, at this time. Freeze the occasion, arrest it from flux. Thus removed, store it. It gains value.

At this point, there's Blat. But here also. And that's Blat, too. Time is finally flat enough, to have Blat everywhere.

A STUDY IN BROWN

BROWN'S BARGAIN WITH THE EARTH ON EQUITABLE TERMS

Brown made a bargain with the earth. He would live as long as it let him; it would live as long as it had to. Earth accepted the bargain Brown had the short end of it. The deal was favorable to both, thanks to Brown appreciating his slight proportion through the lens of modesty. The earth returned such favors, in its confident and proud appraisal of its immense strength. Such was its power, as to make such power seen and succumbed to by Brown's accepting modesty in his role of slight partaking. His short time seemed enough. Earth would know many Browns.

HOW BROWN LEARNED CAUTION'S PROTECTION

First, Brown lived life innocently, as an all-out venture. His fingers and toes were singed, for the blast from the open fire was all-too-hot even at the most moderate distance that timidity could declare and reticence could enforce.

That taught Brown to be cooler in his approach. Life's open hearth was fine and cosy, but not when the warmth actually stung, when the fire snapped at him and broke off to bite him like sprays of foam. That was bringing life quite too close to home. So he grew his own reserve by developing a detached temperature formula to preserve his composure and under fire to keep cool for all that. It would keep him alive that much longer.

ON WHAT STREET IS BROWN WALKING?

Brown had free choice, in an American democracy, *where* he could be publicly walking. To exercise this choice is not always easy. He was about to cross an avenue which would lead him to decide at a forkway whether to go down Eighth Street or to go down Fourteenth Street, both of which would equally lead home, but presenting two opposing routes of a long time getting there in his transition, two emotionally opposed thoroughfares, presenting a personality problem as to what sort of man Brown was by which one he would choose. His character was presented with a critical action, to clarify the *inner* direction that most swayed his inclination. He crossed the avenue, and went toward Fourteenth Street. He went down it, and saw his mood objectified.

What had he avoided in Eighth Street? What was he gaining by Fourteenth Street?

Two different sorts of people, altogether. Fourteenth Street was the rough working class who struggled at the rudiments of survival. They were inside life to such a toll that something like art had no place in it, and was regarded to be superfluous to all true ends. Did Brown feel *like* these people? Or so *un*like them, that he could observe them with free detachment?

He'll walk down Eighth Street another time, What did the Eighth Street crowd mean? All things, truly. And so did the motley treaders of Fourteenth Street. Brown was arbitrarily differentiating, since categories are the streets and avenues for thought to cross.

And who was Brown? *All* categories. He contemplated himself, in the rich multifold of his journey.

THE WELCOME ACCEPTANCE OF RELUCTANT RENOUNCING

Brown figured out that the world has too much of absurdity, and there was only one minute to move the surplus out of the way. Should that feat be done, then clarity would replace ideals. But before Brown could act, the minute was up. Then he stripped off his hope, rain-soaked and an unbearably heavy burden. Brown had the whole past to revert to. He'd be a free-breathing fool at whatever his turning direction should be. He fit his role so well, it immediately assumed his character. Only an academic difference between them.

THE REVOLVING BROWN AROUND HIS MARTHA FIXATION

Martha was Brown's weakest point; or, to put it another way, she was his weakest link in the chink and armor of his amorous chain of being, the daisy chain of life's innocent love for the loved one. She refuted all his theories of innocence until, one by one, he had to follow her in spurning them, She led him bitterly from open unsuspectedness into joyless hopelessness. His love soured into hate for her, so sour that the only sweetener would be revenge. Iron cruelty would replace his former open rosiness. He had been taught that by her, and the teacher must get the lesson in full from the resentful pupil.

BROWN BEING CHANGED

"The sun is getting unruly," said Brown in passing. "On its account, my brow has perspired itself into sweat, my armpits are damp, my chest is soaked, and for a companion I must put up with my own discomfort, being split into a twin bubble by the sun's power to impose the double vision."

"Take a bath," Martha advised. Her chilling retort left him bound in cakes of brown dirt. The temperature dropped. The sun went out. He was now someone else.

BROWN STAGNATING: ALL FOR A WOMAN

Brown took stock of himself: what his age was, his height, his weight, and other categories he was human for, that summed him up to be a man. He deliberated in his calculations, to plot a campaign. He was bent, he was determined. Item: He should improve his life: let that priority be assigned to his agenda. His prospects should be improved, that he should graduate from bum to figure of employment. That should get him in good stead with Martha, who, like any maiden or polluted dame, was very hot on security, should it ever come to marriage between them, which of course why should it?, for it was a tradition with her to spurn him all these years, and the custom made her more conservative in all these days of fouling his ardor with rejection. So, just to spite her, a bum he'd remain. For, you bet, *two* could play this game. Why go out of his way for the ungrateful wench? His shiftless inertia would keep on stalling his development. Middle class ambition had to be rewarded with Martha's hand. Barring that prize to spur his enterprise in a fever of venture, he'd just stay as put, and only mope in despair of hope. Martha, a woman, had driven him to this impasse. He sighed in the role of a wounded romantic.

BROWN'S STUPIDITY DEFENDED FROM THE POSITIVE MENTAL PROFESSOR

"I'm firmly and unshakably of the opinion," a college professor acquaintance heartily maintained to a downcast Brown, "that you really are intelligent." Followed by a slap on the back, the hearty kind that a politician gives to a businessman crony over brandy and cigars. None of this reassured Brown, who remained in a self-skeptical funk. He sat humped-over in his dejected chair, while the college professor acquaintance tried to pump some confidence into Brown's puny frame of morbid pessimism that breeds self-defeat as easily as a fly breeds other flies in the egg-laying season. Then Brown insulted the well-meaning professor; saying, "We're *both* stupid."

An indignant purple flushed over the professor's face; "How dare you include me!?" he lectured Brown.

"I'm sorry, I meant only me," Brown retracted. "I called you stupid for having called me intelligent, which lowered my estimation of your estimations. You mustn't deprive me my modest humility. It's all I can flaunt, to compensate for the deficiency of anything else. My intelligence was never developed, being smothered by so much ignorance, like a fire in a fireplace smothered by a congestion of logs that take up the whole hearth and prevent air from fanning the fire up. Life has reinforced my stupidity, which is now rigid and unwieldy. And so I'm forbidden to entertain any mental glory. You behold in me the splendid example of untapped potential, a dormancy behind a never-opened door. For this, should I rejoice?"

The professor agreed not. Brown had displayed himself in a repulsive light, and the professor was disgusted, since no one should be his own self-disparager, it was so undignified. Optimism was a courteous social gesture, and Brown had violated the code with a plea for disrespect which the professor couldn't help but oblige. Brown was an infectious demean-er, so the professor hurried away, abandoned Brown in the darkened room, ran out and shut the door. Brown was left alone, and recovered some pride with the professor gone.

His solitude went on brooding. "He accused me of intelligence. That placed him in a judging position. It towered him over me, by condemning me with his flattering appraisal, as though I were his colony for him to dominionize over. I hate these social comparisons. I'll be what I please, and resist his elevating. I deserve my lowliness, it's the sole right I have left. It gives me a base to view things from, it forces me to be looking up if at all I'm to see. I won't brook any professorial interference."

Brown retired into a stupid daze, where he loitered vegetatingly, relinquishing thought altogether but for the kind that drifts in. It was his own stupor, no one could deprive him of it. It was life reduced to the par of a breathing stone. It was elementary subsistence, without having to overplay his powers and top his fundamental level with crown layers of pretense that played false with his honored least. His least was all his minimum, and therein was some truth that wasn't far to fetch. Better this little worst, than some big far-fetched froth he'd have to play up to.

He tired of pretending intelligence with a party of professors and professionals who kept glibbing from a brittle surface and clever insistences. Brown would stay low, and not parade far from his depth or strut to convention. The stupid, but honest, life.

THE POPULAR MARVEL OF THE COMIC STAGE

The soft-shoe routine, from tap to toe, was Brown 's vaudeville stunt. It brought the house down. It drowned the audience in mirth. They clamored for more. Brown hogged the stage, until it writhed in the animated tune he had rhythmed it with, and the spectators made a chorus of stamping feet, and their clapping palms hurt with delight, for even their applause fell in nicely with Brown's stampede of harmony that run out and crowned the night with joy like the Bethlehem occasion of a Babe's birthday. He had them eating out of the open soles of his feet. He danced a melody home on their ears, that they would always hear.

KERMIT'S BIG NATURE ENDS BROWN'S WHOLE BEING

"By nature, I am what I am," Kermit boasted to Brown. Brown digested this, but his only simple comment was, "That's natural enough." Then Brown saw fit to add, "Naturally, it covers my case as well." Kermit took this in, then comes out with a nervously protested worry in a tone meant to alarm the world. Brown's attention strays; and Kermit angrily pauses, grips Brown by the arm, forces him to listen, and repeats: "I'm more natural than you, because I'm me *and* you." That did Brown in, and only Kermit remained, his nature throbbing with the devoured addition. All Brown's files and correspondences now devolve to Kermit: his identity cards, passport, and other legal tenders of being. Those who have discontinued affairs or other rungs of business with Brown, see Kermit. Kermit, just off his sweet meal, *needs* expanding. Brown will bring more his way, than just Brown plain.

Brown gobbled into Kermit. Kermit the more Kermitized, for such a sweeping intake. Nothing—certainly not Brown—was alien to Kermit's bulging nature.

But where's *Brown's* nature? It's gone into indirect play. Nowhere *precisely* in Kermit, can Brown be located.

Takeovers annihilate. In the new compound, only the conqueror is in evidence. Those vanquished cross into history, to be abstracted by speculation. The charcoal of thought traces back Brown's fire.

[Note: More Brown can be found in Fables at Life's Expense *and* Life's Tumultuous Party. *He is not to be confused with Blat, although Marvin, in a recent email wrote that he has* "a secret hunch that both were surreptitiously modeled after [him]."]

EVERS IN NAME ONLY

His name is only Evers? That's hardly impressive!

The *man* fills out the *name*, and gives it a shape.

Oh. What shape does he give his name?

His own. It's what *he* is.

What is he?

Evers. You have to *experience* him, to gain the essence of *that*.

Then his name is inseparable from what *he* is?

They're as close as one thing.

But I know an entirely *different* character who's *also* named Evers.

Well, then the name is applied to a different dimension. In *my* man's case, Evers takes on this one particular man's meaning, distinctively unmistakable: Evers is Evers.

Is that all the name he has?

No, one comes before it.

Ah! The plot thickens! Will my knowing it broaden his character still deeper, with each detail unmystified?

No, you've got to know *him* first, and savor *his* implications, before the extended ramifications inform his name with what poignant impartings they ever intrinsically yield.

Oh. But for the record, what's his first name, anyway?

But your ignorance of *him* would render it irrelevant.

Even so, what is it?

But aren't "Evers's" vibrations sufficient?, considering you haven't even *met* the man yet?

No, I'm intrigued with what I *don't* know, whose enchantment holds me in thrall to its unexposed darkness my mind's lantern has been lit for.

Why haven't you asked me why I *did* divulge "Evers," but withheld the preceding name? Couldn't *that* be charged with significance?

Yes, an *add*ed puzzle. Why did you choose to reveal "Evers," but not the *first* name?

It's as much about the man I cared for you to know. I selected according to some limited, but dark, intention. My bestowal was regulated by some inner purpose.

Along what lines?

It's inner to *me*, even; I can't fathom my motive. Evers means something to me. Then you put *your* construction on what I say. Evers is given air.

Quite individually so. The more we discuss him, whether by negative terms or positive, the more rounded is Evers in his personality's apparent presence, as I "see" him. The timbre of his voice, his skin texture, coloring of hair, prevailing climate of expression, even the distribution of his soul's weight and the balance of his extremities psychically considered: all these, "Evers" conveys, by nominal connotation. Never having encountered him in the *actual* sphere, I can envisage just what "Evers" means, according to the lights laden or engraved to your implied interpretation. "Evers" is your verbal creation applied to my comprehension. Through you, Evers is as I know him. I'm satisfied.

But what if you're wrong? There may be more to him, or less, or different.

I hardly care. This research you've inaugurated me into, has reached a certain degree of finding, and will now cease. I have no regard for accuracy fortified by pointed scruples. The *image* contents me. Thanks for it.

The existence of Evers—it holds a reality, for you.

My version of his identity is as real to me as his own life is to him. *Has* he a life?

He does in fact exist.

Good. Now there's *some* basis, for what *I* believe.

What *is* your belief?

In Evers. He exists. Details can go hang themselves. I know him. How are his three children?

Very well, but one is ill.

Too bad. And his job?

It's all right, He expects to retire in a few years.

Well, he's getting on. And along, too.

Yes. In fact, I have an appointment to meet him next week. A matter of dinner. His wife's cooking. Good apartment they have. Might bring them a present. Any sentiment, or regard, you might want to send through me? Evers is relaxed about non-acquaintances. I'll relay what you ask.

It's too casual, since I formally don't know him. I'd rather keep anonymously clear of the picture.

Don't be bashful. He's a friend of *mine*, and *you* know *me*.

Don't involve me. He *is* a stranger. Or, *I* am to *him* through our using of his name. That's too one-sided, and unequal, a relationship.

Pretend he's a myth. How would I cheer him up, through you, then?

That perks up my confidence, and I *do* feel sorry for him.

Good, you've dropped shyness. Any message?

Yes, Tell him to be.

He *is* that, already: my telling would be redundant.

For his *own*, in his own right, go let him be. I take a disinterested wish that he thrive and suffice. His image will hold up, in me, whatever befalls *him*. Something *of* him is in my mind. (False or true, what's the consequence?) The rest, like him*self*, is incidental; and rests outside my province. No further liberties will I take.

So you own a bit of Evers.

Mentally, I do.

And Evers; as he *is*??

The *name* of Evers is what I know. That *settles* it.

On so little evidence?

(With increasing boldness, even audacity:) What more matters, in his allotted scope? There's more known or unknown in the world or above, than the minor Evers portion. Proportion thrusts Evers into shrinking perspective. *He* may egoistically expand: that's his business. For me, as I'm not his obsessive biographer, or private secretary, or even his actual met acquaintance, I know what I want to know; and let the matter drop.

This will disappoint Evers.

(With arrogance:) Let it. If he's central to my universe, I'll take the trouble to *be* him, myself. Already having *me*, that's not worth my while.

Evers has his own grounds.

Granted; I won't trespass them, because I don't wish to. I could crash into his home, knock down his tumbling door, any time. I claim what I wish, and know as far as I care. He's fortunate I don't invade him.

(Alarmed:) He has a right in his privacy. You wouldn't publicly violate it?

I own his *name*, don't I? His name is in my head. That *my* property. I *respect* my property: I'm not only encroaching on it.

(Decisively, but defensive:) In the *actual* Evers, you have no share. *Physically*, I mean.

(Cocksure, like a Western cowboy strutting in boots, the bar bully boss:) *That* doesn't daunt me. I think I'll confiscate Evers; and take him over. This whim has just come over me, and titillates my fancy.

Evers has been too aloof from me. Who is he insulting? I'll teach him to shorten his distance. I won't leave him with an identity left!

(Dramatically begging:) Please leave him alone! *(Contritely:)* I'm sorry I started this.

That one name was all I needed. It started me off, I took over.

It became a tyranny. The nature of a name is that it must be *filled*. At length, you *did* fill it, to your own purpose. You took what bare armature there was of that single name, and constructed all the padding around it, to fill out the sculptural destiny you assumed. It's *your* fabrication. You're content, and beyond that won't investigate. What you've made is your territory. But it was *taken off*, on the Evers name. The *name* you own. But no claim on the *person*.

That *person*!? Who?

The real, the true, Evers. *(Pause, letting that sink in to full impression.)* Are you he?

No; I'm plainly only me.

Die you *begin* as you?

Yes, and I'm still me.

Then don't presume, Who is Evers?

Evers?

Yes.

Someone else.

Fine. Now your priorities straighten out. No blending or confusing. A territorial overlap is a toy you can't afford, nor any aggressive expansion. Stop twisting. Settle as you.

Then take the name of Evers away. I'm plagued to a haunted distraction by it.

It means no harm. What can a name do?

And what's the *first* name, be*fore* that demon one?

What's it to *you*?! Are you *nervous*?

I don't like it.

What?

Evers.

The name?

Yes. Is there a person behind it?

Yes, so don't hustle the person, by trifling his name. Hands off.

My *mind* is on.

Turn your mind off. Then "Evers" would blink out.

So would everything *else* go.

To purge *one*, means to rot out the lot. You're diseased. Evers is your cancer.

Malignant?

(Tender, softly evocative of innocence and dove-like mildness, in a tone of extreme gentleness abruptly changed from the harsh, preceding lines; even pathetically pleading:) Evers? Oh, if you only knew him! A *harmless* guy!

[Editor's Note: Marvin likes to borrow his friends' names for his fictional characters, for example in the novels Inside the World: As Al Lehman *and* Women, *and* Tom Gervasi, *and here with Bob Bonazzi and David Evers. By contrast, Blat and Delp are imagined in both character and name.]*

BOB BONAZZI

BOB BONAZZI AND I, AT BALL

Let me keep playing ball with Bob Bonazzi; exchanged youths, get renewed, when the ball passes hands. I throw, he catches, the ball is our youth. Keep that ball flying. It's our passage.

CATCHING WITH BOB BONAZZI. AIR-FILLED LIFE

The ball is being thrown. Bob Bonazzi catches it. More proof that I threw it, loses its necessity. Now *I* catch it, when *he* throws it. Life's an alternating current of this completed cycle. Life is the *throwing* of the ball, its *return* throw, its periodical catches. The mere ball itself, is not what life is. Life is what's *done* with it, in the air.

Our life is in the air. We're ball-aviators.

The ball is only a mere thing. It's too material to matter; except when put, always, into play. Always.

Our catches punctuate at intervals. Friendship's ball is flying, life is in the air. What's between us has to be renewed. It's flying.

We soar into heaven's ascension. That's life, from the ground.

Bob Bonazzi with his arm, I with mine. Our hands nimbly ready. The downcoming ball going up again. Flight. Life. Ungrounded.

A KICK OF FRIENDSHIP

Bob Bonazzi kicked me in my buttocks, but in a purely friendly way, causing shock waves to tremble through my pelvis, issuing in painlets overall through my extremities. As the vibrations shuddered to a stop, I already pre-explained to him how forgiven he was, for his kick was in the nature of an emphatically friendly gesture. I doubled over, to show that pain and friendship were virtually on a par. The pain hurt; the friendship didn't.

Then he fed me, from a bowl of glistening food. I was eating, now, at pleasure's source. Delight's sauce quivered atop the food. I felt good, all at once, all over.

He showed me where I could sleep. As I lay there, in the spot suggested, he sat nearby, tinkling at the piano. The latter responded to the nimble ripple of his fingers.

I was asleep, dreaming of him. I had known this Bob Bonazzi, but when? Long before I had ever met him, of course.

I woke up, and breakfast was ready. I feared his foot kicking me again. Quickened by friendship's little ripples of terror, I kept always my front to him, so he couldn't kick from behind. He co-operated. The day alertly sped by, that way.

THE BOOK-DEVOURED BOY

Someone's parents, before he was born, hired a prophetic ghost writer to do a complete lifetime autobiography. Publication coincided with the subject's birth. He was weaned according to the book. His education and experience were controled by the written word. Any inaccuracy resulted in a costly "author's alteration," and a new edition of the autobiography had to be sent to press. He grew up in conformity to prescribed style. One day, as a young man, he sat down to read the book. (His parents were out of the house somewhere.) He grew so absorbed in the pages, so hypnotized by the style, so woven in with the pattern of detail and event, so intrigued by character development, that he merged with the pages, and the book and he became one. The parents returned and found him asleep on the library shelf, half-way open. They closed him, and were depressed by the failure of his remaining life to conform with the text.

THE BITTER POET'S BILE OF POISON REVENGE ON HIS SPITEFUL LITERARY CRITICS, IN LIFE, IN DEATH, BEFORE TIME COVERS ALL IN A MERCIFUL NEGLECT TO MANURE THE WAY FOR NEW DISAPPOINTMENTS IN THE PURSUIT OF PRAISE AND FAME FOR MILKING THE DRY MUSE OF HER SORDID TUNES IN TINSEL DESECRATION OF HER FORMER BOUNTY. A TALE FOR POETS, TO HEED.

An embittered old man, who never got the recognition he felt he deserved, put a mental cube of mind poison into each adverse literary critic's bowl of bileful soup. They were all killed off, proving the power of the mind. But young fledgling literary critics were hired in their respective steeds to fill up the vacant posts. To a man, as by instinct (homing or otherwise), these replacements printed unfavorable critical reviews of the old man's poetry. He killed them too, and the waves who succeeded them, more furiously than he wrote his poetry, till he also was dead and his poetry finally could be forgotten. Which it was, but then, in an irony too late, there was a big boom and revival of his work. But where was *he*? He was stewing just where the old literary critics were, in a cauldron of bubbling mentality perversely poisoned. There was no longer any personal revenge to take, for damnèd public insult. He was lionized in life, were he only there to join it.

Then his poetry faded away, and never had a revival. It joined *him*, poisoned in death.

Moral: Write poetry at your own risk. You have no right (or rite) for complaint if no prosperity, no posterity, accrue. You'll rue it. Prepare bile. Pour poison, *be* poisoned too. It's all impersonal. Fame is a trick. You never deserved it, anyway.

HE REFUSES TO READ SOMEONE ELSE'S BOOK. IT'S *HER* BOOK. HE'S NEVER EVEN MET HER. HIS RETICENCE RESPECTS PRIVACY, EVEN THE PUBLIC CORRUPTION OF PRIVACY GONE BOOKISH. HOW GROSS, THAT SHE HINT HEAVILY AT FAMILIARITY IN MARKET PRINT. HAVING NEVER BEEN INTRODUCED TO HER, HE'D LET HER PRESUMPTION FALL DELICATELY UNREAD

Have you read her book?

Oh no, I wouldn't presume to read somebody else's book.

But she *likes* people to read it.

She wouldn't mind if I read it? But it's her territory. I wouldn't be caught trespassing. I have too delicate a sense of propriety, than to trample roughly over her property. No, no, it's *her* book. Let it *remain* so. My reading would be an act of plagiarism. I wouldn't *dream* of imposing.

But she *wrote* it for it to be read.

But I'm a total stranger. Surely she intended it—

—for strangers. Such as you.

That was rather forward of her. We were never even introduced. She doesn't care *who* she's exposed herself to! That smacks of private desperation, to be so publicly promiscuous, so indiscriminately personal. She shows all the familiarity of a begging bum who petitions any passerby and openly invites contempt. How *dare* she fling her book at me! Let her first at least meet me. She's won my distrust, but not my readership.

She doesn't need you. *Others* will read her, and gladly.

Read *her*! That's obscene! You mean, read her *book*! Her *book*! Dirty laundry, hung out in ragged print. For *any*body to paw over! Well, what's for anybody is not for me! Let her peddle her wares, in the scum-topped market. Let her court the quick vulgar eye. Let—

But her book is an account of how flowers get their colors. Isn't that an innocent topic?

She's probably being symbolic, under the cloak of symbolism, *any*thing goes! Art covers up for the hideous criminal act. But I see through this clever front. Enough to veil my tender eyes, from the siren claws of unclad intimacy. Between the book's covers, the deeds of the monster are spawned. A flower's colors! What bold begettings, from a sweet innocent trick!

THE EYES' PILGRIM VENTURE

As I opened a book, it showed the stacked shelves of a self-complete library. I busied myself in lipreading the first word. But I borrowed it out of circulation so long, I lost my annual subscription. In a gesture designed to defy the mismanagement of institutionalism, I unlearned my ability to read. This entitled me to the world visibly seen.

A common sky, one huddled Mother Sky, crowns the rising efforts of all the total buildings erected by international architecture. Smoke issues from some, as a winter offering to the suspected abode of gods clustered in heaven. The uniformly blocked streets wear the walking paths of people's pedestrian wayfare. Those intermingled directions carve a complex heart to distribute the central outposts of a city.

When the clouds conjoin, a web of rain secretes the closed weather. The sun's vegetable appetite has been denied its extra dish of happiness; its smile is warped by a daylong fast, as the fangs of a thin diet molest its disposition to roll out flesh. Man's gifted umbrellas turn their convex blindness to the sky's dropping ocean. My house is an old-fashioned cave. On the walls are illiterate words, on whose wisdom my scanning dumbness has fed. Racing backward down the corridor of evolution, I encounter green slime, the sea's crop of spawned germs, each replete with a single cell. I greet these faded ancestors, but so dryly had I polished my cosmopolitan lungs that the fish uttered guttural tones and swam by, devoid of recognition.

So abandoned by my birthplace, I rejoined the strides of progress, and liberally sprayed mathematics in fine powder on a speedy telegram that delivered itself on a pair of wings into what collected heads remain on my monster brother's teeming body of mankind. And who shall replace my well-established modernity, once younger births are recruited?

As a boyish prank, I plant a tree and water it with my own sap. The seeds drink down deep, and a tribe of dancing branches goes drunk into the sky, letting twigs of merriness pluck an April load of leaves. I climb up this rising column of bird-blessed rhythm, until I spot words on a passing signpost strewn along a suburban stretch of some celestial citadel. Below, my forgotten body, which my hurried speed had abandoned in the steepness of its ascent, stuck bound as a brown root, going no place divine.

(SOME REMARKS ON EXISTENCE, OF THE RANDOM PHILOSOPHICAL VARIETY. BY AN ANONYMOUS COMMENTATOR ON LIFE FROM THE HUMAN POINT OF VIEW (NARROWLY, HIS OWN). NOT MEANT TO PROMOTE WISDOM. MEANT HARMLESSLY; AS ONLY GRATUITOUS COMMENTS.)

It's hard to exist unless you *do* exist: then it's easy.

Existence, carried to a fine art, becomes living.

Living, carried to a fine art, becomes . . .

A fine art, carried to living, alters the living.

Life is subject to influences, both from without and from within. The former are called external influences; the latter, naturally, internal. Surely from this semantic base . . .

A bacteria is smaller than a tree. Logic can grow from both.

A man is only on earth once. That's his whole life. Yes, but what a life! Ask him, he'll tell you—he'll complain. He'll boast, too. He'll justify himself, rationalize his existence. He's got to square it—with himself. He's got to like himself—even through self-hatred, self-contempt, regret, remorse: it's all got to come out, somehow, in a way of retrospect whereby he can sit up and say (pointing self-ward), "That's me. Say what you like, I ain't got much, but still, I got my dignity. No one can take it away from me. It's all I got. But it's enough."

Is he apologizing? What is he doing—I mean, trying to say?

THE GAME OF ALL-PLAYFUL SPORT

Life is strife;
And sports are strife in games of play.
Life is sport's sport;
Or sport is to play life's regulated game
In formal rules at a lower stake:
A posturing spectacle
Best performed
By a seriousness just as intense
In concentration like art,
But unlike art, being pure event:
A loss and a win.
Reversible, at the next match
Given the sufficient odds of chance
And excellent application
By the other team's athlete
At the similar-ruled arena
By the uniformed fair exchange
In grounds of decisive strife.
Life: lit up excitingly
To that mock ritual: sport.

A BANAL INTERVIEW, WITH A CONCLUSION BASED ON THE FOREGOING, LETTING LOGIC HANG LOOSE FROM THE PRIOR PROCEEDINGS LIKE A BELLOWING FLAG FROM A BRAVE AND FORWARD MAST

Who do you represent?

My company. I work for it.

Ah, what field are you in?

The manufacturing line.

And how's business?

Not at all bad. Slightly seasonal, right now.

Of course. You must expect such things. We're not perfect, you know.

LIVING LIFE AS THE SOLID BASIS FOR THE LEGITI-
MACY OF LIKING IT

Look what a fine world it is! Taken all in all, there's nothing ad-
mirabler.

What in particular of it strikes your favor happiest?

The best thing I like about the world is life. And the best
thing I like about life is itself.

But can life be *liked*? It's too big to be "liked," that is, to be
subject to one of our affections. Its size is so big, that it's all we
can do to *live* it. And living something, since it's bigger than "liking" it, is thus a compliment more in proportion to the great big
thing concerned.

But I have been living it. *Any* living thing can live it. But liking it is special—it gives evidence of a higher faculty: to marvel,
to appreciate, to be exhilarated by it with the zest of spiritual
discernments, consciously. We should single out and encour-
age what's special, not what's common. *Living* life is what I have
in common. But *liking* it involves the use of more extraordinary
faculties

All right, like it; as long as you're living it.

I promise to stop liking it, if once my living of it ceases.

Good. You're at least that much realistic of what primar-
ily comes first by cause and necessity, to give priority and so
avoid undue sentimentality that comes from liking something
before being it. Do all the liking you like, on the strength of living as its base. For living will have provided for your liking, and,
accounted for the affectionate substance you may draw upon.
Your structure is built from the ground up; therefore indulge,
on top.

THUNDER BREAKING IN ON SLEEP. THE RIDDLE OF BEING AWAKE.

All that thunder last night! It kept interrupting my sleep so much that it turned out that my sleep was periodically interrupting the patches of thunder, for the thunder had more the stability of a continuous regularity than the disconnectiveness of my sleep which that thunder would periodically punctuate.

How much sleep did you manage to get last night?

I can't figure that out, because I wasn't awake at the time.

But when *did* you sleep?

How should I know? I was asleep at the time, so I can't tell.

But weren't there windows in your sleep for you to look out from?

Yes, but they weren't going anywhere, those windows. And they were flashing with thundering lightning, thus obscuring the tranquil perspective of a clear and broad panorama all deeply detailed in the field of repose.

Thunder was invading the sanctity of your slumber?

It was pattering my fitful bouts of wakefulness.

Did dawn clear the skies of that wild chorus of static, so that all was serene for the winged twitter, the feathered flutter, of ode-beaked birds in lovely pastoral entry?

No. Dawn was a mess. Besides, I was asleep at the time.

Really? For how long?

Being asleep at the time, I hardly remember.

Does sleep grant you immunity, impunity, for gross observational negligence?

Sleep declares its own moratorium on the wars of consciousness. Soft oblivion folds up the knitted sleeve of care. Troubles and fits of anxiety are lacquered and varnished with unruffled layers of lovely old forgetfulness. Fear, trembling, worry, misery, and other undesirable sensations, are all eased away, in a blurred comfort of gainful loss. For in sleep, we're lost. Such loss as restores all we have, when we wake.

Then what's the point of sleeping, if that's the case? For we're back where we were before.

It's *necessary* to sleep. Otherwise, we get too sleepy. So we sleep and get our energy back. Then we can face our terrible woes, the awful liabilities of that ill-kept business, life. We can grapple, again. With the round forms of living thunder. With the gross shapes of thunder-in-the-round, that dog our heels and snip and snap, from every angry direction at once; in this strife of the wakeful land. Before oblivion captures us, in its sweet mercy.

What will it be like, to sleep again?

Hard to tell. I'll be asleep, to what goes on.

Will you forget before you even experience?

I'll unremember the nothing remembered. May no thunder bolt in. I'll take my death in short, sweet previews: interwoven with fits of grateful waking, and long drafts of deeply-brewed consciousness married to the out-of-window world. The likely old world. Kissed ripely, to my forming mind.

The mind unasleep?

The sleep-tossed mind: with wakeful penetrations by the world, that insomnia-monger, that tunes our awareness to that fiddle of sad old chords.

What's it like?

Who knows? I'm too awake, to tell.

HOW UP SOON BECOMES DOWN, FOLLOWING DOWN'S RESURGENCE OF UP, AND SO IN ALTERNATES OF PENDULUMITIS EBB BY WAX

(You Have to Be Up to It to Delight in the Beautiful. When You're Down. It Shoots By and You Can't Nab It. That Lowers You Even Worse. But Don't Worry, You'll Recover. It's a Cinch You'll Soar to the Heights Once More. And Fall Bottomly Again, in this Bouncing Course.)

(Characters: enough to make a dialogue. Any more or less would unfit the roles. So two will do, to keep the margin straight.)

Life is so uncertain. I'm confused.

Art will afford a brief cure. Catch a beautiful object, in a comprehensive glimpse. And you've caught a well-designed whole, all in one breath. A shell will do, or an old church, or a composite person in one deft act. Or a row of flowers, or a very good painting. That's the stuff will fix you, when doubt and skeptitude, and other afflictions, happen to disturb you. In nature or literature, you'll find consolation. Now go take my advice, and seize the fleet beauty.

My senses are paralyzed numb. Melancholia has depressed me down, into a lowly state of mood. Art quickens me; but I have to be quick to flag it down, as it whizzes on past, in its unbroken stride that the senses must snatch at once, latch onto, and instantly grasp. Beauty swiftly fades me by, I'm caught awkwardhanded. I stumble, and the valued moment is gone.

Then you're pathetically unequipped, your capacities dulled, you're too sick to fall on the prey. The cycle is against you: you need alertness to win a beautiful minute. But that minute was too quick for your detection. It's over, and you're still where you were: feeling low, and misery. You can't get up.

Any reviving remedy can you suggest?

No. Let beauty be at a lull. You'll feel fuller later.

Then woe!, for what I must endure.

You're *complaining* now: a good sign. Soon, you're cured.

But how?

Your zest was rested. Watch it store up, with superb renewal: and shoot out, sharply restored, in the ardor of a new heat. And life will prance with beauty, while you dancingly choose. As you blaze with darts of delight. And take rich beauty by the tail, art and nature's worth at a double shot, for all your horde. And the wealth will pour. You'll soak and ooze, through each informative pore. And divinity will shed its treasures on you; by the store. And great your acquisitive joy: by the blinding moment of *experience*, not in paltry *things*.

Thanks. I can't wait.

Don't die before.

My revitalization has begun its soaring instant. The booming explosion has just prickingly begun.

Make room; Give it rein. Its tremoring scope shall broaden. It consumes space. Start up. One surge, for the tumultuous uproar. With beauty to bulge feasts at the end; and the spirit taken frenzy of, when ecstasy heaves its pressure out, and the big bolt is shot. An ordeal will exult you. Then watch it subside.

And I'll fade to be as before?

Lower worse. Bottomed in the dungeon down subdued into suicidal apathy, the despondency of all gloom. Immune to relief. Poor you. But first will befall the best. Speed through that, on your way to fail again.

REPETITION, AND REVERSAL. ALL DIFFERENCES DIVERGE FROM SAMENESS, AS SIMILARITY CONVERGES FROM DIFFERENCES. THE EXTREME OF SIMILAR IS IDENTICAL. THE EXTREME OF DIFFERENCE IS SEPARATENESS. THE EXTREME OF EXTREME IS THE EXPECTATION (NON-SURPRISE) OF IT.

My human body isn't functioning efficiently.

It's not operating up to its best form?

It's been making excess motions that gain no purpose.

Wasteful tics, motor sputtering, repetitive acts like compulsively checking the lock, or returning home to see if the light had been turned. out, and the stove off, and papers put in order, obsessions of fruitless endeavor, that achieve nothing but waste time to secure temporary reassurance on pointless points in a circle's void, excessive effort of no practical consequence, acts chained out in cycles of reiterative isolation, symbolic peering under chairs to see if you left anything behind before moving on, ritualistic gestures like making sure you didn't forget to do some vaguely superstitious propitiation of the gods; walking at a certain gait, avoiding arbitrarily selected signs, playing a geographical game with rooms, furniture, or street landmarks, rewashing already clean dishes, taking care beyond caution of avoiding imaginary germs or nonexistent dangers, being antiseptic and going back to wash your hands again with more soap after accidentally bumping them against a dirty object that rubbed off some contamination upon perhaps that deliberate contact: are these what you had in mind?

That's the way *my* catalogue would have been recited. How did you get such uncanny insight into my malfunctionings and wasted motions and nervous implementings that serve against myself by diffusing energy and dissipating my random impulsive charges of overorganized ritualizations and unprofitable schemes of intricate complexity barren of goal? Are you similarly afflicted?

Yes, how did you guess? Because all your symptoms seemed so familiar to me?

Yes, and we're equally slaves to neurotic whims that squander our forces and neutralize our drives by the symbolic acting out, blindly compulsive, of deeply-rooted, unmanageable conflicts that come insistent to the surface and demand sublimationary outlets and weirdly odd channelizings of those dark devils beneath.

Should we seek out a psychiatric cure? Therapy is expensive.

Let's analyze ourselves further. Of what are we the victims?

Of some inner plaguings. We're stiff and rigid with some need of imposed order. The mysteries of chaos may subconsciously worry us. We can't endure confusion, so we enforce some arbitrary rules which we ruthlessly execute however irrational, enacting rites to unoverwhelm ourselves in the hands of fatal forces beyond our comprehension, to which we submit, but transcend by exaggerated servitude. Our deeds have a hidden meaning.

What meaning is hidden?

Too hidden to tell.

Maybe *that*'s its meaning.

We must act more spontaneously. With more freedom.

"We"? Who are "we"?

The two of us.

Two!? But there's only *one*!

Which one?

Me. *(Pointing at self.)*

Then who am I?

You're my dialogue partner, within the same me.

What if you're *mine*?

Same thing: only in reverse.

Are reversed things same, or different?

Both at once . . . We're a duality.

Are we?

Yes. *I* am, anyway.

And me?

You're my other me.

But what if you're *mine*?

Same thing: only in reverse.

If in reverse, it's different.

We're being repetitive.

You're being repetitive. *I'm* being repeated.

Same thing—only in reverse.

What's in reverse?

You—you reverse me..

But you said I *repeat* you.

Same thing—repeat and reverse—same thing—only inside-out.

To *me*, it's outside-*in*.

Oh, you. You're necessary. What would I be, if you didn't repeat and reverse me, and act as my "other?"

What other?

Mine.

Yours!

Who else?

Mine—only in reverse.

That repeated me.

Can't we ever get out of this?

No. One needs both.

But *which* both?

The same one.

Which same?

Us.

"Us?!" But that's *me*!

That's you—which is really me, only in reverse.

Then you're primary?

I'm *only*: but you're my "other?"

But if I'm "other" to your "only," am I really necessary?

I'm essential; you're necessary. Essentially, I need repeating, and reversing. That's where *you* come in.

Then I'm *used* by you.

You *are* me: you *complete* me. You're more me, then I am.

What am I, for myself?

That's for *you* to determine: who *are* you?

THE SELF-IDENTIFICATION OF AN HONEST NARCISSIST

Man is dignified, and I'm here to prove it. My friends will all back me up, in their loyal lifelong devotion to me; and I'm just as good to them. Of my many outstanding virtues, perhaps they are equally all deserving; none better than the other. My strong-points are a constant comfort to me, and I utilize them to the full rung of their capacity; and each day I polish my weak points, so that their brilliance shall not be noticed. I do consider myself complete, and am not alone in thinking that; others quite agree.

Life is said to consist of goals; I include myself in that category, I'm conditioned to expect happiness; yet, being fair-minded, do not begrudge its absence. Nor am I alone in this. I'm generally the average; but vastly superior; truly in my own class, peerless.

Profit being my motive, I prosper; yet does it avail me nothing? No. I'm here to get all I can; with the result being considerably less. Am I discouraged? Yes, but I plod on.

You may take me as a sample, a classical illustration of myself. Who would serve better? None, but I. At a great personal sacrifice, I consent to contain all my characteristics in one integral whole, a structure, a unit. Yet I surpass myself, and am entitled to what remains; which consoles me for the stubbornly mediocre qualities which reputation, guided by a few ungrateful enemies, insists on stamping me as: yet my greatness prevails, scorns accusations of being illusory, and gains main strength, vital well-being. I'm all I can be, and what I can't be, I do. This leaves me no time for idleness; I'm busy with constant frequency; and continual application; by which I achieve much, with my scanty time. Others flare up and notice: cries of approval and respect have me for their object, and I gracefully nod, with appropriate modesty. Do I appreciate it? Yes. There is something infallibly human in me.

WHAT IRVING WANTS OUT OF NEXT LIFE. (TO RE-
PEAT AND SIMULTANEOUSLY IMPROVE THIS ONE.)
HOW UNREASONABLE OR EXORBITANT HE IS! BUT
HE MAY GET AWAY WITH IT; HE'S CERTAINLY NE-
GLECTING A LOT IN THIS ONE. TO MAKE UP FOR
IT IN THE NEXT. DESERVING IT IS NOT THE QUES-
TION. HE HAD THE AUDACITY TO MAKE THE RE-
QUEST AND EXPECTATION. THAT'S WHAT MAY PULL
HIM THROUGH, OUTRAGEOUSLY BOLD—FOR WHO
WOULD DARE TO REFUSE? SO THERE'S IRVING, GET-
TING IT. IT'S MAGIC TO US, SO WE HOLD OFF. TO HIM
IT'S NOT; SO HE STEPS IN.

In his desire to live his whole life over again, Irving got careless about the one he was only living now. He regarded it as a rehearsal, not even a dress rehearsal, for the "real thing" which, in repeating, would correct and perfect.

As the correcting and perfecting were bound to be, this *first* round of things didn't matter too much: it would all be fixed up later.

This furnished Irving with excuse not to make much of now while it was going on. "Now" anyway didn't count, really. It was a "warm-up" for the real thing later. Consequently there were no consequences about current action to consider; nor was he responsible for his responsibilities—for there were none, now: remedies would automatically come, atoning and rectifying, in the next life. All would be redeemed. So why bother?

So he was carefree. He never worried. He was calm.

And so slipshod, with sloppy negligence. It was his contribution. It would give his next time around some solid undoing, remolding, to do: a lot to clear up. Yet he would be living this life over. But with what polish, precision, consummation! Yes,

he'd be living this life over. And that would entail superb uphol-
stering, for having "let things go" this time. He'd be living it all
over. But what a finish he'd apply, a trimming, a pruning: that
would renovate and repeat at the same time! Irving asked for a
lot. He may just get it, too.

NUMBERS AS THE PRIME AGENT OF SOCIAL COHE-
SION, SEQUENCE, CONSECUTIVENESS, ESTABLISH
UNBROKEN CONTINUITY IN THE BROAD HUMAN
BOND. MONETARY AND SCIENTIFIC GEOGRAPHY
AND HISTORY UNIFY PEOPLE TO A SYSTEM, WHICH
MATHEMATICS LOCKS IN PLACE. WOE TO HIM
WOULD VIOLATE THIS EVER-EXPANDING STRUC-
TURE, LINK BY LINK, THAT MEASURES CIVILIZED
TRADITIONS TO THE KEY OF ALLNESS WITHIN EACH
ONE. NUMBERS STABILIZE OUT SEPARATENESSES TO
ONE PAID COIN.

I know a guest who was so greedy, that he demanded his thirds
before his seconds.

But that's a mathematical impossibility. Numerical sequence
simply will not be abused that way.

But his demand was a request. You can demand or request the
impossible, but that doesn't mean that you will *achieve* it.

By "thirds before his seconds," you mean helpings of food, re-
fillings of plate? And he asked that of his dinner hostess? You
nod yes. Then tell me, what reply did she make, his hostess?

She said, "I'll give you second helpings *before* your third helpings. Your greed shouldn't interfere with the number system."

That's the reply *I* would have made, had *I* been the dinner hostess, and not she.

You approve of her mathematical orthodoxy?

Approve!? I *venerate* it!

Why are you so concerned with numerical protocol, when
greedy gluttony and bad table manners and abuse of hospital-
ity are the *true* issues at stake?

They were at steak? That's my favorite delicious food. For steak, I would *also* have distorted numerical sequence. With *that* at stake, who wouldn't?

You're an ill-mannered oaf, and a greedy pig.

No, I just have a taste for steak.

But your *second* helping of steak still has to come *before* the *third*.

Oh, you're so fussily finicky and picayune and petty and pedantically precise and obsessively accurate and technical and official and formal and bland, about the exact order of numbers. Numbers serve *us*; we don't serve *them*. If numbers are instrumental to my desires, my desires come first. So I'm justified in ordering my servants about in my own fashion. If numbers *serve* us, I want third helpings before seconds.

Why not be a tyrannical despot of a dictatorial emperor, while you're at it, and demand that the moon and the tides and the waves should defect from their natural principles and come under *your* arbitrary sway? You make a power play of unreasonable will, to meddle with the *order of things* and disarrange traditional procedure which civilized human logic has historically collectivized in standardized social acceptance by lineage of cumulative legacy. Suddenly you and your anarchy appear, to let all that fall to chaos. You lack respect. One, two, three, four. Eat consecutively. Follow time's procession, and get fat on heaps of steak. But get fat *orderly*. Be geedily ill-mannered *orderly*. Be unforgiven, but *orderly*.

Yes, I'll *order* my hostess about: that's how *orderly* I'll be. And numbers don't count. Somehow, they just don't add up. I subtract them, from my regard.

What would the world be like, if more people like you get born?

It'll unworld itself of stiff rigid customary codes and inflexible modes frozen to the ice of custom. People like me will loosen things up. We'll rearrange, and turn things over, upset established formations, and begin all over. We'll have a whole new numerical system: the number's up, for the old one. Fall as they may, the digits will assemble concepts unfounded on automatic acceptance. We'll stir things around. The people will be a new breed. They'll eat when and where they like, with their own "how." And invent their own sums, any which way. Let banks crumble down, and finance fall to rot. Let's abolish numbers. They boss us about. They rule our lives. Let's revolt, I say. That's a revolting notion. I won't buy that.

It's not for sale. Nothing is, any more. I banish all prices, from the economic structure. All costs are outlawed, all salaries and fees and taxes and interest and other such obsolete fractures. Numbers and money tyrannize. Let's go back to bartering, on a different coin. We'll wreck all measure, all standards, all uniform systems. I'd joy to destroy. I'll fracture the number chain, and let the links fly apart. Consecutiveness chains us in. Let's break through, and open up. A non-mathematical human image: not reducible by formula. That's my non-ideal, if you wish.

Are you an anarchist? Would you govern by absolute chaos? Would you rip social threads, and dissolve the bonds of humane unity? Those are dangerous sentiments, and give you the bad name of a rebel. You're punishable, by group action. The mass will swallow you up, and pulverize your dissenting lump. Numbers keep the tribe intact: safety and security are founded on the numbers. If you're anti-number, you're a nothing—or will be levelled to nothing, by your destruction. The collective avenges its internal enemy. You'll be ground to dust. And reabsorbed, to the basic elements.

GLUTTONY, LUST, COVETOUSNESS, POSSESSIVENESS AND DESIRE'S LEGAL DISAPPOINTMENT

I like anything I can get my teeth on, in the way of food. This includes edible things, also.

I also like whatever I can get my hands on, if she's a pretty woman.

If not, my hands don't necessarily come off: habit keeps them on.

It also keeps her off. Thus a contest, a conflict, ensues.

She wins, legally. And I lose, illegally.

Is it fair? Certainly not. But complaint has acquired ail the fuel I needed, to really flair, and I'm sufficiently upset. So much so, let me try a good meal.

Ah, that's fine. But is it really mine?

THE WOMAN REALIST AND THE MAN IDEALIST. A DIALOGUE

(Woman:) Why do you seem so angry with me?

(Man:) I want to get to your soul, but your face and body are in the way. And they're *wonderfully* in the way. And exasperatingly, because I'm impatient for your soul.

What would you do with my soul, if you got to it?

I hardly know. I've never been there before.

Do you want to *join* it?

Above all, yes.

My face and body *seem* to lead to it, but they carefully conceal it.

Why does it *need* such elaborate and attractive concealing?

My soul may not *need* what it has. Not everything needs what it has,

Sorry to be so assuming. But what *is* your soul?

The inmost me part of me.

Is it accessible to me?

No, only to your soul.

Then let our souls join.

Our faces and bodies stand guard and are fast in the way.

Then I'm frustrated.

Let's *pretend* our faces and bodies *are* the souls we so covet. That'll our task easier.

But the mutual self-deception involved! No!

What's your solution?

Anger and frustration are closer to the solution than what you suggested.

But why not regard our faces and bodies as *emblems* of our souls?

I take the soul too literally. So emblems are out.

But the soul can *only* be shown by symbols.

That's inadequate, for me.

You're too stern an idealist, a perfectionist. It inhibits, prohibits, and confounds you from working *anything* out.

Then it's no deal. I abdicate.

What from?

From these games. I want God directly.

By what method?

(Angrily:) No method: I said *directly*.

What has *God* to do with our *souls*?

(At the bottom of his patience:) Need you ask? God *is* our souls!

But what about us?

Us!? You mean you and me?

Yes. Don't you care for *us*? Or only, via God, for our souls?

You confuse me.

You were *already* confused. I'm just defining and clarifying what it is you're confused about.

I feel lost.

(Tenderly:) Don't. There's always *us*.

(In a lost, childish, absent tone:) Us? But are we real?

Too real. That's why we argue.

It's such a problem, being real.

At least it's a real one.

REGRET FOR PURE VANISHED YOUTH

Inside every sixty-five year old woman is a twenty-five year old woman trying to get out.

You mean trying to get back in.

No, she's already in there—been in there for too long; not been expressed recently enough, not given enough voice, enough scope, to turn out manifest.

To turn out man-for-sex?

In essence, that's it. An old woman is lonely. She was used to attention and love, long ago, and set her standard to it. Her standard hasn't been met lately, She envies what she *had* been—meaning *who* she had, who cared for her.

It's sad. We get less than our previously built accustomed share.

Our expectations have had to become reduced. We're reluctant to have gradually given way.

Sad, imperceptible withdrawal—from love's sweet little eternity, that youth-protected truth: wherein, securely, we momentarily outpierced anxiety with delusion-borrowed assurance. Since then—

"Since" is all our sin.

TO SOMEONE REMEMBERED MORE THAN MET

All the time I saw you, you were disappearing. You were so young and so physically attractive, that what were my chances to have any luck with you? What powers could *I* throw into the bargain? Yet I did compel your attention, because I talked to you sympathetically on the topics you felt most personal about. But that couldn't go on forever, could it? Your attractions multiplied. While mine waned.

Then, your eyes grew impatient. You were being lost. The tides were sweeping you away, and for consolation your image grew more vivid. I've been nursing your image. Has it balanced out for me more in pain or more in pleasure? It has peculiarly combined both. The same as though it were really *you* with me, and we tangled as real persons.

THE STANDARD LAMENT

I'm still "game" to bait and be the bait of what's always been the opposite sex. I'm available, I'm looking, I'm starved. But I'm less desirable to prospective partners, simply because I've become middle-aged. Why must I suffer for a crime that wasn't my fault?

It used to be that I was magnetically attractive; I had successful love affairs. That glitter of my previous spellbinding is now muted to ordinary dross. Yet I entertain an increased eagerness, in proportion to my diminishing luck. Frustration has thwarted me into a bitter and unattractive desperation.

Which will worsen. My situation's plight will get eviller yet. I'm not through aging.

THE LOOK THAT LACKS THE ACT, AND IS CONTENT MENTALLY JUST TO GO BACK. SEX BY CONCEPT ALONE.

I'm looking at women more academically, now that my active lust juices have become inactive lackluster aridity. Whereas I used to be ignited by a sway of proportionate haunches, and planned to lay siege to their sole possessor with the aim of co-possessing them on a temporary free-rent basis, now, I merely note them, merely for visuality's sterile sake alone, observing with dry academic detachment what used to be the provocation for a swift course of a seductive line of action. I stop short, now, of wooing the woman, content just to look. The look used to be a beginning. Now, the process stops there, save for dream imaginings, using nostalgia's wealth of material, on instant recall to embroider fantasy's current prop or pretext for instigating the retrogressive onrush of similar evocations to the lush, voluminously curved reminder on display there. Sex is in my past. Seeing a new woman ignites old impulses. I'm mentally inflamed. But my genitals don't leap out. They stay put. I dream, instead.

WHAT HAPPENS TO THE WANTER IN HIS WANTING?: A) IN HIS GETTING: B) IN HIS NOT GETTING. ALONG THE WAY, WHAT GOES WRONG?

My desires don't find fulfillment anywhere. The curved fruits I wanted though pastelled to Rubens, were waxen to the touch.

I desired that girl. She was an imaginary being. When I came over and reached out, she was like a windowed scene. I did all the looking I could, and all I could cause was her vanishing.

Pale dreams. Money is a coin of another realm. Money is by working. But most working consumes it.

Oh what to want. How to be able not to get, and live with the not having. Deprived long enough withered on its own vine, desired snows out its indifference. Heated longings led, in the end, to a cold lack of results. We who desired, remain.

THE GROWING CHILD NEEDS NOURISHMENT, NATU-RALLY

In her growth, she devours people. *For* her growth, she devours people. She sucked this one's brain pap, that one's head juice, and that one's mind brew. Those she devoured are still intact. But she's growing—till when? All growth has a limit; so must hers. Then *she*'ll be devoured, but by whom?

A DREAM JOB UNABLE TO FIND ITS APPLICANT

I have a vacancy in my dream. Would you like to fill it?

How suitable am I? My modesty shirks.

You seem type-cast tailor-molded for the role. Never did one particular person seem so personally personifying of a dream's ideal abstract which invariably never meets the concrete embodiment of its image in an actual realistic person. Your occurrence was by chance, in coinciding with my internal projection of you into the apt choice of focus that precisely answers the soul's dumb cry. The opportunity ripens your consent to balance outwardly my romantic spirit's vacant depth that constitutes a suitable opening for you, if you're interested.

I do need a job, and was about to report to the employment agency.

Save the agency fee, and enter my firm by direct application. You'll fill the post beautifully.

But I'll be a wage slave, bonded to you in service, with a position of such responsibility to your interests that I will have left my own freedom behind. No, I turn down your offer, in kindness and duty to myself. I know how well I'd fit your spiritual void, and answer your dreams' specifications, for I'm well qualified to be the fulfilling companion of your soul's lonely cravings and absolute imperious demands. I'd be a serviceable function in you; but for the privilege will have relinquished the entity most integral to my own apportioned fate. I can't afford the sacrifice. I'd rather be me than yours. You can understand that.

I had been prepared to make concessions in *your* interest, as well.

That's a charming offer on your part. But I turn it down. Merging would disrupt the economy of my being solitary. My structure would dissolve by union with you. It couldn't withstand forsaking its independence for your dream's benefit. So don't ask. I've turned you down.

It's sadly tragic: you would have been the only one. A perfect opening in my dream. Which now closes forever.

THE MORAL USE OF MAN, REAPPRAISED

I began on a high note, and the professional man frowned. I sustained that high note, despite the professional man's increasingly evident disapproval:

"The world is tinkling with fairies, elves, cloven spirits, spriteful imps, and other basic types. Dewy cobwebs are to the foggy dawn what inflated mushrooms are while night still rocks the mercies benevolently. Godheads dot our mountains, like goats that dislodge pebbles from the steep spires of wonder in their scampering bursts.

The panes at Christmas are a cheery cake of frost; and the red berries splash with drops of mirth while the spiky leaves of ivy stir their darkening green poison to pursue the infant's blood on points of pricking capture. Materialism screams with fits of wonder, and chemical surrealism leaps up from every disturbing stem. Froth pops bubbly intervals, like beer with sparkling aspirations to wine. The twists of nature perform these unlikely tricks, to entertain the serene phantom of Possibility."

The professional man scowled bitter wrath; without breaking stride, I went on in blithe defiance:

"I submitted my nightmares to the wild scientist of the mind, who analyzed them into joy. I coughed my painful glee and cheeked the pillow stained white by the bulb of reminiscence on the bed's beaming table-side which the switched lampshade could barely subdue. Romantic whimsies clashed, and girls split into fragments on haunching gyrations. Between knee and elbow, the prize sizzles, and our goals turn sexual. A cascade of girls had made me physical since adolescence reared the stallion's thunder. Who had pleased me most, from skirts bursting with pink? A composite myriad of girls, lashing their hair in tumbling coils or curls, had stampeded my pressed body over twenty-five years. And each one had earned the same tool. Most Don Juans have never been to Spain."

The professional man seemed puzzled, as I gaily romped on:

"To recount the meals I had would burst a table's seams under such a groaning horde. Dirty plates stack the meal's end."

He glared at me with open hostility. But I was in full stride, in the flow of uninterruption:

"Let me summon who I like the best. Her legs at length from below would reach the body's haven, like two slim tugs that join the bulging liner on symmetrical side-hinges. (Is the ocean only a whale's surface dream?) Why was love's delight reserved for the spastic festivities of night?

"As I chase the mental miracle, sleep closes over me on two sides, like twin waves that crush the helpless gull. My voyage has always been a drowning."

I confided these thoughts to a professional man. He professionally examined them, and said that normality had been outraged. My penalty was to be a freak in the averted eyes of more *common* man. Why wasn't I a *healthy* kind, or average? Conformity must begin with the mind. Then it spreads to bodily behavior, and permeates the rest. "Too late," it was pronounced, in my rather individual case.

"I'm closing the case," the professional man now frankly consented. "Walk out and dream what you can't help but feel. All that otherwise could be prescribed by me as a worldly man of practice, would be lost on you and abundantly in vain. Don't endanger my professional career, by making a laughing mess of my feckless treatment. I wash my hands, and dismiss you, free."

I walked out of his brown-panelled office. The day was attached to the tips of various twigs, like a laundry sheet that the wind has caught.

Miraculously overwrought, seemed this world's stupendous normality. Beams bit into me, from the slanting sky.

Clouds were twisting the color's alphabet, and the ink was dripping into my eyes like the vengeful mirth of syrup dislodged from a glistening battle.

Heaven's streak was a spear in me, quiveringly clinging yet still, being hurled.

My breath must rival all the fields that wonder has filled. All aspects of my given life met inside the mind. The mind was God's plaything. Why fear breaking so beautiful a toy? Games galore should spread from it. Like a Christmas gift, its childish duration should be tested fearlessly and each crack and stain would only release a glowing sentiment. I was convinced that the folly of fear would alone destroy a greater Folly's glorious glories. Was courage needed, to be happy? The ultimate goal of discipline is to bring Indulgence to a frenzied art, as the cross-paths between all likely extremes. I would romp mentally, and so fill my spirit's soul. I thrilled with elastic motion, and knew how well applied are nature's human resources when the will soars its way to free heights and dipping plunges for the depths that correspond. In that guiding light, life at least has a chance: to rescue itself from the stern *professional* piety.

I could hear his despair, that professional man's: "Another one lost," he'd crack, while pity was bleeding from his lips. "Let the fool go," he's conclude, with professional sagacity. His contempt I deserve; but his pity was too hard to take. I'd smear his face with it, were we ever on civilized terms to collide as savages used to, and men in unctuous bouts of war waged to the modern rhythm.

What shall I do with passion, instinct and intelligence? The best economy is to give them employment: that's what they're there for.

TALKING TOO MUCH TO PREVENT DANNY DOING SO. BUT NOW *I'M* A DANNY FOR *OTHERS* TO PREVENT LIKEWISE.

I was afraid that Danny was going to talk and talk and, boring me, never stop. I was determined to prevent this. Here he was, approaching me. Already his mouth was beginning to open. From past performances, he'd tend to dominate our conversation completely, unless it truly actively opposed.

I wouldn't let him. So *I* talked. *I* launched the offensive. It would be the most powerfully effective measure of defending myself, warding off his verbal pressure force. I took an initiative and held on, not daring to relinquish it for fear that, once he'd counter with a violent burst, the vehemence of it would perpetuate its never-endingness. So I used his own weapon in an over-compensatory anticipatoriness, rushing him off his auditory feet, or so to speak.

It worked. I tied up Danny's tongue, with my rushing gush. I kept it up. He never recovered. Annihilated, he had to take it.

In the process, though; *I'd* become Danny. Others would then have to do to me, what I'd just done to him.

I'd let myself in for it. Fearing to be the victim, I'd turned victimizer. And invited retribution, retaliation, by others in their own defense. Retribution and retaliation for what I'd never done to them, yet, but for what they'd fear I'd do, based on my inglorious reputation for having paralyzed and enfeebled poor Danny: whose former aggressive loquacity was now, deplorably, my own responsible identity, making me the dreaded figure to be slain at once in all-out assertive warfare, using words as bullets. I'm vanquished, then, as Danny's vanquisher. The successive overturning, then, of two Dannys, brutally silenced.

TWO MEN IN A HEAD-ON EVASIVE POWER STRUGGLE

Already we're in disagreement.

But I haven't said a word.

Your very silence has condemned you.

But what opinion of yours has my silence seemed to contradict? Certainly my silence was of a neutral, unoffending sort, hardly given to contention, opposition, and disputation. Are you *inventing* our argument? If so, what contrary views have brought it about? Or are you just angling for discord?

You're wrong, whatever you say. And that proves it.

There's no avoiding getting into a headlong conflict with you. You're picking a quarrel; but *I* pacify for peace. So my strategy will be this: whatever you say, or even think, I'll fall into quick agreement with it. I'll give you nothing to fight against. I'll smother you with my concord.

If there's anything I detest, it's *appeasing*. Will you stop it?

You're *determined* to find fault. But I'll politely oblige, and not once resist. I'll go soft on you. I'll melt into consent. You'll find that there's no contest. Then you'll give up your attack; and perhaps like me a little bit.

Your very weakness is an affront to my strength! I despise you.

And I agree with you. Only too well, I do.

I reject your obedience. I want you to struggle.

I willingly acquiesce. Treat me as you wish.

Stop your non-resistance. Show more fibre.

Only in your command. I'll humbly oblige, in everything.

I order you to disobey me.

Yes, sir.

Then I've won?

No; you haven't.

THE UNPAID DEBT. TWO LIVES DRAINED BY IT. THE PARASITE, DEPENDENCY, CONSUMES BOTH, AND GROWS BIG BETWEEN THEM. BOTH LIVES SUCCUMB, TO THAT OBESE GODDESS.

Somebody owed me money. (I had loaned him the sum in a weak moment that he caught me in. He detected that just then, psychologically, and only then, in just that set of particular circumstances and my emotional conditions at the time, could I have consented to lend him what he asked. I've regretted it ever since.)

Well, I wanted it back. Enough time had elapsed. More than any decent borrower's interval. I wanted to get it over with. I didn't like him anymore. Not *because* of his borrowing and delay in returning, but I disliked him *any*way, for his *own* sake. It was pure, disinterested dislike. Yet I was bound, obliged, in spite of all my inclinations to the contrary, to keep in contact with him, to phone him periodically; for the loan was hanging over me, I wanted it quits with, to get it over with, to release me from the bother of still not getting my money back, from the burden of his indebtedness to me, and from the tedious insincerity and hypocritical repetitiveness of pretending to be phoning and contacting and even sometimes seeing this man for the sake of any pseudo-friendship with him or liking him or some mutual interest.

Just let him return the loan, and the case would be closed, I'd be free of ever seeing his tiresome face and "indirectly" asking for his return of the money.

I became desperately dependent. He was my obsession, my sore point, my nemesis—all because I couldn't afford, or was unwilling, to forget the debt and let it go unpaid.

I phoned him at increasingly small intervals. It was dragging on *his* nerves, too. How he must have hated me! How I detested him!

But why didn't he just pay up? To get *me* off his shoulders? To get some peace, from my incessant nagging, constant badgering, phony "hints," indirect mentioning of his loan. I pretended to want to see him for *his* sake. And he kept up *his* end of the bargain, by pretending to friendliness with me.

Neither one of us could let off, we were shackled, to each other, that way. Like Siamese twins of undying enmity.

He *could* afford to pay me back. But he got into the ritual, or fetish, or whatever, of just not doing it. This prolonged our anguish. We were in a headlong, mortal strife. Neither would back out, for pride was at combat. Weakness was in conceding: my saying "Forget it," his saying, "Here it is." No compromise. We were fierce. We were deadlocked. Relentless. In stubborn passions. Years went by. No one gave in.

He hounds me: I phone him all the time. I plague him, remorselessly. He haunts me. I haunt him. We have this mutual need. For that, we need each *other*. It's our joint identities, now. He's not himself, without me and his debt. Nor am I me, without him; and his owing me. It's now a stalemate. We're locked. In perverse style, we're *married*. Is *money* our root's evil? Or is money an excuse? Does dependency have its own *independent* life? For dependency is bigger than us both. It sucks us, from two sides.

THE METAMORPHIC PERSISTENCE OF PROBLEMS IN THEIR PROTEAN PROFUSION OF SHAPES

(The tone in general must be consistently and comically hyperdramatic.)

All the ways I have of losing my dignity!

How self-insulting of you! Cut them away!

No, I need them. They're the only cures I know for an inflammation of the pride.

(Exclaiming in discovery:) That's your trouble! You're too proud!

But I *need* my pride: it somehow restores my dignity.

(Disparagingly:) Dignity! *Fight* your false dignity!

But every remnant of it is necessary, to prevent my looking ridiculous!

Oh, how absurd!

Yes, the logic of it escapes me.

How *unreasonable* of that hidden logic!

Will reality rescue me?

Ah, when those veils of fantasy lift!

EYES VERSUS EARS, WITH NO WINNER, ALL ON THE SAME FACE: A TRAGEDY. TOLD IN TERMS OF WAR. BY WAR FOUGHT, LITERALLY.

My face once underwent civil strife; hideous to report. It was split by internal warfare: strictly a domestic matter. It was a dispute between my eyes and my ears. I tried to arbitrate, but all suggested resolutions or compromises were turned down by one or both both parties in the faction.

My ears regretted being on the same face, with my eyes, and threatened to leave the union as rebels whose grievances were kept dissatisfied and whose dissent was softened by no concessions on the part of my offending eyes. My face felt torn or split, on an elemental sense level, at its essential but contrary roots. The union threatened, I declared an open emergency, with drastic measures. The contending factions fought on, and all federal injunctions were futile. My face was out of order. How could I pull it together again?

My ears insisted on a hearing; but my eyes couldn't see it that way. An eye for an ear, equally could have been plucked out as mutual offenders, in vindictive retribution.

My eyes asked why my ears couldn't "see the light;" my ears replied that the arguments put forth by my eyes were simply not "sound." So it raged, each being deaf and blind to the other's insistencies. Their stands were irreconcilable, and they grew further apart, dogmatically headstrong to a fault.

They couldn't face up to each other's demands. Neither was ahead, but the head was losing.

Strategically, the ears had the advantage, being so positioned as to outflank and surround the closer-together eyes. This advantage was offset by a disadvantage, on the ears' part: those ears were too divided for effective communication and coordination; whereas it was easier for the eyes, ostensibly, to act in unison, being closely juxtaposed.

The eyes acted to split each ear from the other, to divide them from each other's supply and to isolate each to a remote corner where it would be rendered helpless and taken prisoner. But the ears warded off this stratagem, for their intercommunication system proved essentially sound; and the eyes couldn't see their way through to divide the enemy ranks. This costly war threatened to wipe out the world of my face. It wore out the face of my world. I just couldn't face it going on much longer. It was effacing all my valued institutions. On the face of it, it was endless. Yet the end was "in sight" or was that "hearsay?"

My ears wouldn't hear of surrendering; my eyes couldn't see *themselves* folding, either. My nerves hurt. This stubborn, solemn struggle was affecting all my features, in neutral confusion.

I was wracked. I must end it, but how?

The ears threatened to pull out of the union; but I was deaf to that proposal. Nor could the eyes illuminate this wretchèd scene. All was senseless, scattered.

To *preserve the union* would be the *sensible* solution. In the War between the States, the final result was that the two severed parts were still lincoln together for the cleavage to mend. I thought of my face as a unity. To save face, I would have to keep it that way.

Other faces sent reporters to report back on my civil war in their respective foreign journals. While I was distracted by domestic problems, no alien face took advantage by aggressively butting in. I was grateful for the other faces' forbearance while I was trying to keep my own house in order. I would have been vulnerable to belligerence from without, just then; with an averted face (or *inverted*) I prayed thank-you while my internal turmoil spread its pale misfeatures all about. I wouldn't have been able to face up to a foreign invasion. The ears and eyes of my soul were on home matters, entirely.

Discord! It's hell, with a split head. It gave me a headache.

The rancor of my ears for my eyes; and of my eyes for my ears, was like a persistent drilling. I needed it like I needed a hole in the head. My head was likely coming apart. Its disputants just couldn't come to their senses.

My methodical defacement was plaguing pockmarks and minefields to mar the former handsome harmony by which I had once been featured. Would it mark me for life? Disfiguration would make a casualty of my battlefield. There are even *worse* features in store by war. All life would disappear, on the face of my globe. Would I become my own death mask? I must head off further disaster.

I was ravished, and sacked, in brutal hostilities. Brother against brother—a more than moral family disgrace. Harmony must be restored at the head—or all, including below, is lost in the enveloping holocaust. The wound was sinking slowly poison into the body politic. I was a tribe that had lost its head—a riot untamed, but fanned on, in divisive disorder from on high. This factionalism had started at the top—what's to halt its ever widening, toppling wake, that blazes a most destructive trail? I must step in, and restore the semblance of sanity;—alas, the gap was a breach, and my heart's loyalty was wrenched asunder, as member blotted out member, in a ruinous conflagration. Legislatively impotent, judicially powerless, administratively feeble—I was plundered, destroyed, inch by inch. I'm going under. Head first. Crowned, in the sinking ground.

THE VITAL CURRENT OF LIFE

Born in the morning, the child was man the same night. By dawn, he was dead.

The mother lived in the usual time. She wept to have created, in her fertile years, just that one day and night of life. She'd been short-changed by the destinies of duration; was she generatively deficient?

She hungers for her husband, requesting another child. But his sperm has been used up, and he bears no capacity.

But his one-day son, who'd been manly the night of his born day, had impregnated the neighbors' sneaked-in daughter; there was hope for dynasty.

A POLITICAL PROPOSAL. A BIOLOGICAL VETO. A HUMAN ACCEPTANCE.

Death is awful, we ought to abolish it.

Yes, the very *idea* is repugnant.

More so than the *reality*—which would be well-nigh *unthinkable*.

We ought to politically outlaw death—as a human menace and an ultimate mockery of our dearest-held values and our life-prized ideals. A political act *could* do the trick—if the weight of *all* our politicians stands solid behind it: not just *our* politicians, but those of far-flung nations as well. A world-wide campaign, to make death a criminal offense and the very bane of humanity.

But isn't politics itself, even on a global scale, completely helpless in the face of simple biology, which simply will not be appealed to?

Biology is the culprit: were it not for it, we wouldn't have this death-nuisance on our hands.

What do you propose?

To go to the *heart* of the matter: reform biology.

Easy to propose; hard to bring about. The most elementary facts of existence, which lie within and all about us, are outside our control. It's hopeless, I'm afraid. Death will not yield to political pressure. It will reduce our efforts to a pitiful folly.

Then we'll just have to sit by and submit?

Not till later. Meanwhile, let's live, a bit.

"GENTLEMEN, LIFE IS DEAD." "LONG LIVE LIFE, THEN. LONG LIVE THIS DEAD LIFE."

I wish to bring something back into the present, to dislodge it from its fixed and frozen position in the past. I would like to have it appear anew—it doesn't oblige, and what I wanted turns into a *hurt* want, not a want full of the health of hope. But I remain wanting—it never leaves me, but turns sour inside. Sweet hope has fled. Bitterness, and then mellow. Mellowness, renunciation: harbingers of forgetful ease, and the deep desireless affair of death. *Wants* don't die; only the total organism does. The best cure for cancer known is the total death, by another cause, of the person who might be afflicted with it. Such solutions don't console, they're too stark to sweeten the potion. Sweetness has its place in life: but life is bigger than that. Big enough to break in two (not like a self-reproducing amoeba, but a thing that's ended useless by its breakage). Life had wanted. Unconquerable life.

GIVING OUT, BEFORE THE POWER TO IMPART (HOW-EVER IMPERFECT IT HAD BEEN) IS DEMOLISHED TRACELESS

Knowledge enters the head, but the head dies with the body. Does the knowledge join its head and the body in all that death?

But before that death, some of that knowledge found its way, however diminished, diffused, or refracted, to other heads via writing, speaking, or doing. Somehow, the dissemination, in however a form, before the "too late" barrier was de-constructed. How much leaked out—in code or guise, by distortion or symbolism—before the body closed down the intelligence with the extinction of its individual light?

Convey. *Then* go away. Divulge, however partially, or however unenlightened. Make an effect. Cause, before you're ceaseless.

UNTEMPORARILY UNDERGROUND

Someone died. So for an epitaph, this was engraved on his tombstone: "I wish I could walk around, and not be here." Onlookers pitied the man who was represented by these words. "He has the right notion, his wish is courageously commendable, but his sense of practical realism is nil. Put him down as a mere ineffectual dreamer," they criticized. Their words were prophetic, and true: that man hadn't lived up to his epitaph; the worst had come to be. And would remain, enduring, outlasting hope. The epitaph would be washed dull, and dimmed unreadable, by earth's permanent elements.

A MAN FOR WHOM HUMOR NEVER TOUCHED UPON HIMSELF, BUT CAUGHT FIRE UPON ALL ELSE, IN ITS MERRY *EXTERNAL* BLAZE

Has he a sense of humor?

Only on things outside the peripheral of the closed inner circle of his known egocentrality.

Oh, then he's self-humorless.

Quite: no humor about himself.

Then he can't see himself humorously?

Not at all.

He can only laugh at outside things?

Yes, and more heartily, since he can't laugh at himself.

No?! Why not?

He lacks self-humor, that's why.

He's not funny to himself?

No, not at all.

Outside things borrow the self-rejected funniness?

Compensatorily so.

Did he die laughing?

Yes, but not personally.

Self-solemnly grim did he die his own private death?

He took it gravely, and is all in a grave about it,

And the world outside?

His mirth never stops, over *that*.

You mean *under* it.

Quite so. The surly sod!

A SHOCKING TELEGRAM

Telegrams I hate to receive. It's invariably only bad news.

Only last week, Kermit received the ultimate of terrible telegrams.

What did it announce?

That Kermit had died!

How did he take it, poor fellow?

He never recovered from the shock it gave him.

Did a heart attack set in?

Yes, and it took him away. But there's one consolation.

What could that be?

He's where telegrams will never harm him.

That's an improvement—or is it?

THE STATE OF THE MAN FROM WHOSE MOUTH A TOOTH WAS PULLED

After he died, he suffered an acute toothache. The dentist had to be called . . .

But the dentist's equipment is *heavy* did it have to be dragged . . .?

The dentist arrived with a portable kit. The dead man's mouth was opened by a mortuary assistant.

How ghoulish. I *hate* this post-morbidity.

The aching tooth was located; it could have been saved by drilling the decay out and filling the cavity; but instead it was decided to pull the whole tooth.

Did the dead man protest?

No, he was under anaesthesia and kept numb about it.

What happened when the dentist had finished his work?

The dentist was paid and the corpse buried. Why prolong a short incident?

Who kept the pulled tooth?

It got lost.

What was your point in telling me this whole story?

I intended no moral.

And none was received, either. Won't you untell this story?

But why?

Because it left a distinctly sour taste in my mouth.

A DIALOGUE OF ONCE OR TWICE

This is the one thing I'm going to miss, when I die.
What is it?
A good cup of tea. And a fine cigar.
Oh, those are *two* things.
Then I'll have to die *twice*.
Don't. Once is enough.

Reality & Truth

INSIDE THE HEAD THAT'S INSIDE THE HEAD. OUTSIDE YOUR *OWN* HEAD, IS MORE INSIDE OF *THAT* HEAD. SO THERE'S PLENTY OF ROOM: MAKE HEADWAY

(A dialogue between two speaking self-parts of the same self. They're split only for the sake of separate voices. Once the dialogue closes, those two self-participants will be reformed into one by the silence that ends the need of their division. ((Does speech divide and silence make whole? But a restless silence is not whole: it splits up, into voices.)))

Many of my experiences never took place! (Except in my head.)

Therefore they took place: in my head.

Where does my head take place?

It takes place in the idea world.

Where is that?

In the larger Head.

Is he ahead of ours.

He's our Head.

If he heads us, can we head him off?

No, we're *in his* head. So let's use ours, inside his.

Then where will we be heading?

Heading out.

Out of the Head we're in?

No, out more *into* that same Head.

But aren't we inside it already.

Yes, but not enough. We want to be *more* in; hence out.

REALITY BLOTS OUT OUR LIFE. IS DEATH AN IM-PROVED PROSPECT? ONLY NEGATIVELY SO. BUT AT LEAST, REALITY WON'T RUIN US, THERE.

(Two men in a dialogue. It doesn't matter which two men: any two men. It's what they say, that counts.)

My imagination and the world got into a controversy.

How did it turn out?

We're *still* at odds—there's no reconciling us.

What's the bone of contention?

I *insist* that the world should be like my imagination wants to be; *it* persists in taking its own course, irrespective of my imaginative dictates. The world is independent of my mind—I resent it for that.

What do you intend to do about it?

Complain. What else *can* I do?

You're impotent to convert reality to your point or view? Then what about converting yourself to *reality's* point of view? *Join* your stronger opponent, *merge* with him. Stop holding out and resisting. The odds favor him. Give in, rather than lose out. Let him assimilate you, to his persuasion, which endures, whereas yours is just a passing. Join forces, and you'll be his equal—though on his terms. Partake, then, of his strength.

No, he has enough strength. To add *myself* to him would make it "no contest" when reality faces future opponents like me. I don't want to "stack the odds" and give reality a "prohibitive favorite" rating of invincible might. I want to unite with other reality-opposers, band into a union of dissenters, reduce reality's brutal tyranny over us all. I want the occasional *human* voice to shout back. Reality shouldn't always get its way; its omnipotence is immoral. *Prometheus* opposed the gods; then let *me* defy reality. I'll take a courageous stand, though I lose.

Your futility will only martyr you. You have no force to fight back with. You'll be annihilated with ease. Why protest?, it's only a dumb token gesture. People are helpless. Reality rules without even trying. Best *conform* to it, for personal prudence and your separate survival's safeguard. Reality is so smug, it's not even *aware* of your insurrectionary intent. And if you *did* overthrow reality—do you intend to outlaw tyranny altogether? For a *new* reality will tyrannize, if current power is toppled. It's the nature of rule, for reality to rule, since it always owns all the might. Your "right" is feeble, to question such might. Give in and rest. Find a more effective fight, if fight you must, one where you can control the result. Reality will only paralyze you if you stiffen and balk at its orders. It's laughably one-sided, the contest. Fate is not to be tempted so. Or *you*'ll be fatally lamented, then; and for your grave endeavor, find a grave—a fit and, to a brave fit of folly that no hope lit a candle for. Reality is the unbeatable bruiser, the king bully. It expects your yes. It knows no no. It brutally vetoes no. Don't come under its notice. Know safety's primary survival law: judicious cowardice. Obey. And pray.

Pray for what? There's no hope.

Pray for what reality will grant you. It ignores most wishes, and grants a few.

Which wishes can I impose successfully?

The ones it *wants* you to have. It will honor those; and throw the others back, at you.

I'm a slave, with slave's privileges.

Ask for no more. Reality rations each person's boon. You're on a stringent *budget*. Reality is adamant—you can't *budge* it.

Oh, what a life. Is life only this?

Only. At your peril, seek no more. Stop questioning your harsh fortune. Reality likes *content* customers; the others go punished, in degrees of severity. You can't escape. You're reality-bound. It hems you in, like Prometheus to the rock. Your liver is gnawed at by the vulture. The open wound never heals. This is an unideal world. With a vengeance, it is.

Where can I go ply my dreams, or indulge imagination? Underground? Or in my head?

Reality detects you at both places: its spies have super sight, to ferret out your least sigh, which is taped and magnified for the detection of eavesdropping by the omniscient ear. There are no secrets. Reality is cunning, you can't hide.

No refuge I take? None available?

Reality's unassailable even by harmless tokens of privacy. Through and through you're known, marked accordingly, by reality's network. It's a paranoiac situation, and not the slightest escaping. Your will is a delusion: reality controls *that*, too.

I have no recourse, inner or out?

None. Internally, you're a reality-province. Even your guilt betrays you. Reality has indoctrinated you. It employs you to keep a close guard on you. So you're useless for any other you than the reality-approved one. Reality has marked you with its stamp. You're stamped out, otherwise.

My volition's hardly independent, then. I serve a lifelong jail sentence, in reality's cell. It's closely confining: no way out. That curtails my liberty. What *is* liberty?

The option to obey. No other free choice remains, but that compulsory non-choice: accept reality. Believe in it. It's bad for you. But it alone will do.

I feel restricted.

You are, but you're not alone.

My fellow man all are too?

Yes, so join with them, as subjects all, in thrall all, to reality's reign. Submit mob. And resubmit. No end. Kneel, kneel. Bow, bow. Humble. Prostrate. Before the altar.

That sounds religious. Is reality a *God*, in addition to holding throne in the *world's* court?

Of course. It commands Mystery, to reinforce its *factual* rule. It compounds earth and heaven to a consistent hell. It manufactures more men for its hell: it's nourished by men; and men are bred and fattened for that kill. You're one. Does your mind object?

Yes, but my objection can only be mental. And that's soon detected. I'm punished for a mere thought. Reality is relentless. All is lost in unfair contest with it. I was born to a reality hell. Will *death* find me there, as well?

Reality rejects dead men. Only live ones nourish it.

Then I have an escape hatch. I'm hatched to this hell: but my knell's a contrary hatch, to break the spell. For that I wait in captivity. My release from my season in reality with its term of terror all done, is the solace to contemplate, while this sentence draws out. I've served; and soon I'll go.

But to parts unknown. And with only a soul.

I'll take my chances, on that slenderest of resources. It's bound to beat *here* and *this*, no matter where it is. Death is my salvation. Life *could have been* a salvation: but reality wouldn't have it so. So death's my outlet, for want of a live one. Life was taken over, to reality's kingdom. I'm confined there, and am wasted. I wait for the *negative* chance: a dark release from the unlit gloom here.

This is somber indeed, to think this.

It's being thought *for* us. We're not free.

Who's thinking it for us?

The *reality* of us. *We* receive, and say.

THE ME OF NOW: *PART*; **BUT SELF-CONSCIOUSLY SEEMING WHOLE. I'M THE ONLY, IT SEEMS. AHEAD AND BACK I CAN'T SEE, BEYOND OR BEFORE THIS OF NOW. HERE I'M STUCK. I** *SEEM* **LIKE THE WHOLE ME. I SEARCH FOR LINKS, TO MAKE ME ONLY A PART.**

I only live one life at a time, loath to bite off more than I can chew. I can never see as a "whole" all my series of reincarnations past and to be, since I'm all tied up in this particular "now" life, a narrowing of the attention span, a focusing into the finite.

How do I fit in into the sequence, in the semblance or guise of my present form? All I can see is life in this world from only my vantage-point of this seemingly only life as a being of me on this special earth. "Here and now," I call it. And *me*, I'm doing it. Absolute, universal, eternal—or relative? I can't see before or after this life or my body. My borrowed body, that temporary rented suit shredding into patches now through the neat new knit I once had.

And I ply my life only on one corner of the earth, solely in this city, "my" city. I'm very local. I'm named precisely me, and my life chart or history or case in its portfolio of events (*non-events*, more likely) is all headed under my same name. It's me, here and now.

When was I anything but, or *will* be anything but? Isn't there always an out there, with some other me out there, the me that was the me to be?

A *different* me, of course. A whole series of me's, each different.

But each me detached, divorced, from the preceding me's and the following me's.

Infinity before and aft. *Me*, in-between, caught, here.

BEFORE AS THE MIND; THEN *AFTER* AS THE EVENT. WAS THE MIND "CORRECT"? OR WAS THAT EVENT FICKLE, TO OUTSMART THE MIND? CHANCE, AND PREDICTABILITY.

The history of a worry: Sometimes, you need *not* have worried, as it turned out. The history of a carefree: Sometimes, as it turns out, you *should* have worried. (Too late *now*, of course—the damage is already done. Regret on retrospect. Ah, if only . . .)

Two bad turnings-out, from two opposite causes. Oh well, you can't win. Trouble *could* have been averted, if only you'd been on your guard. Or, you didn't have to bother with all that brooding—it turned out not to have been necessary: energy wasted. Oh well. Who could predict, really? Well, sometimes we *do* predict right. But that's not the point, here.

Who can tell? We make mistakes—or miscalculate. Then we examine the damage—we're wise, afterward. We'll apply that wisdom to *future* "accidents"—which will refute our wisdom. Events change; predictions alter accordingly. Well, what happens next? We *think* we know; and act upon it, by neglecting, or being overcautious. We'll be proven *something*, later.

But proof changes. What should we expect or not? *We* change, as events do.

Yet *we*'re not the events. But *we* change, too. There's some relation, there.

Examine it, and tell me later. I'm too busy now.

I'm forfending something apprehended. Will it be worth my care? And I'm careless about something else. Ah, I should know better.

I learn to be wise. And unlearn *that*, as events turn out.

It's like knowing the outcome of a sporting event. First, let the game be played.

Between games, you will have learned from the previous how to bet on the next. But "learning" is subject to change: at the slightest warning—or too late: you didn't need it in time.

Or you never *were* warned. It's not *your* fault.

Whose is it? Chance. Chance is the winning bookkeeper. You're only the gambler: chance's slave.

But the slave can make a *profit* too. Good luck.

A CONVERSATION THAT MIRRORS THE PING-PONG AFFAIR OF NARCISSISM WITH ITSELF; ON A TABLE THAT MIRRORS, BOUNCE FOR BOUNCE, THE GAME'S WELL-PLACED STROKES BETWEEN A MAN AND HIS OWN ADORATION.

When I phone long-distance I reverse the charge, and when I look in the mirror I reverse the narcissism.

Then that mirror must really strut! But what does it do when *you're* not feeding its image? For isn't it helplessly dependent on you, for all its self-inflated notions?

When I'm not there, it caressingly feeds, lingeringly, on the dear memory of departed me!

But how long can it go on consuming your memory and deriving nourishment therefrom? Surely, it must have already devoured your influence in a few hours. Doesn't it then turn blank, awaiting your return?

I don't know. I'm not *there* at the time, to keep up with my fan club. But when I do return, it's overjoyed to receive me. It just laps me up, like the wet tongue of a deeply panting dog whose adored master has returned from a long trip away. It turns slushy, that mirror. It oozes with wet distortions of my belovèd contours, and drips with passionate contortions of my revered face—which sweats out its deification and rewards its devout worshipper.

Then you haven't given your narcissism to the mirror, but retained it and trained the mirror to dwell not on *its* narcissism, but on *yours*.

But it *reflects* my narcissism.

No—it reflects *on* it. It's like the supplicant before a priest, the humble petitioner genuflecting before its king. The mirror has become your *subject*.

But I'm *its* subject.

Those are two different meanings of the word "subject." Anyhow, you haven't relinquished your narcissism, when flattering your fawning mirror with the condescension of your holy presence.

The mirror merely confirms the "me"ness of me. It instruments my vanity, you see.

As *you* see. What does it give you back?

Me, to my magnification.

And what does it *get* out of you?

Me, to its enlightenment; that it may be so edified, to its burning zeal, by my supreme, original example.

All it does is mirror you. It even *apes* you, gawpingly, and not always to your advantage. You only seem what you are.

What I am is enormous. If what I am supports what I seem, then seemingness lives in great expansion off of me.

How seemly you are, in your eyes!

My mirror countersigns my being, like a bank manager endorsing the check of a client whose account sums more than all his bank.

Then your mirror doesn't give you your due! It should *equal* all you are; not fall short!

I'll scold it. It *must* come up to me. I'll train it, to be worthy.

FOR A CHANGING SELF AND A NEW BECOMING

I said to myself (who's the usual receiver of what I say since he's so close and handy all the time as the constant companion whose presence is so regularly dependable that his absence is hardly ever noticed and when it is then he comes rushing back out of breath panting his pathetic apology and by forgiving him I make him one with me again), "There's still enough of the un-known left for my adventures into mystery. I haven't used up all my experiences yet. Even my *past* experiences are open and not closed incidents. They're open for me to redo them in a new way to find discovery. Life is not known, even while time's pas-sage conducts me to the last half of my earth stay in the body form I have for it. Pools of energy have been collecting in my mind—are they stagnant puddles and weedy rubbish ponds full of festering decay? Or are they oceans of voyage, the fountains of fabulous travel?"

The self I addressed this to was my own. Is that conversa-tional nepotism, or talking-by-incest? Was I being inbred? I confidentially passed the matter on to the self in question, to let *him* handle it. What's he *for*, but to ease my lot?

I got tired of my "self." He apes me too much, can't he be more original? He's my unflattering mirror and the tape recorder that plays me back just what I don't want to hear—the things I had already said. So I fired that self for failing in origi-nality and in the sense of adventure, and in unwittingly being my mocking mimic in his unconscious parodies of me burden-ing me back with overfamiliar essence. I would hire a new self who would *lead* me, rather then follow in a cautious noxia of re-minder. I want to be *led out*. I want a self with initiative—a self-starter, to find paths that would open out and get me away from the misery of my usual me in which I'm so habituated that it's like a drug of sloth and repetition and sterility and sameness. I want a self who would infect me with vital wonder; who would light a spark under my sodden feet, ignite transformations resulting in that I'm me no longer, but someone else with me for a past.

I want magic to unstick me from me so I can squirt away, like a fly from the fly-capturing glue-paper that lures him to be trapped on a humid summer wall in the filthy toilet room of some cheap public place operated for a paltry profit by attracting the drunken poor.

I advertised for a new self but there's no qualified applicant to answer it so I think *I'll* respond to this opportunity for travel and adventure. Who wants to mope around in the old and make a venerable sacred code to its outworn honor? Many's the church that's outlived its vital inner prayer, and with the spark gone remains as an architectural shell or lifeless coat of sacred hallowed skin hollowed out into no memory at all, for the memory's fled to take new life in some remote secular but uncelebrated from afar.

I look for the not-me to address my ideas to in words that are like darts groping in space for a moving target.

I'll converse with myself no longer in single-edged dialectic. I don't want my ideas to fall like rain water upon the sponge-like ocean or like snow evaporating in the sands of an endless desert that sucks up the snow and drains its force but gives nothing in return, till the snow depletes itself and has nothing left for all its spill, nothing to show for the show it put on, its resources all drained like a man's creative sap in a tart's auctioning lap.

I want to get recharged. I need *someone else*—an *outer* being. Someone to answer me no, to challenge and test my offerings, to reply and make me occasionally back up. I need *opposition*, not assistance—defiance, not mere compliance. I need an enemy as much as a friend, for a friend may be leniently unquestioning, and indulge me too gratifyingly. I need the tough fiber of some definite "other" that won't yield when I come against it, that insists on itself and forces me to vacate myself so that

I can take notice and learn. When I return inward, I'll be coming back enriched, expanded, by that outer contact—which will have fertilized me, and started new rivers going.

An adversary sharpens my muscles and brings my wits into mobilization. I rise to his challenge. I'm no longer pampered by my "self," cuddled like an infant by his obsequious "yes." I need stern handling, at the hands of an "other." It will "bring me out." It will expose me to harsh external standards, and dash my pet flunkies that have overprotected me.

I need to come to grips—with the world, that offers no favor but bites me in fair contest. I need to grapple. The servant "self" won't do—a slave makes a poor adversary. An independent outer being will do, for me to come up against. That's the real stuff. Am I up to it? Or made too spoiled, by the lavishings of my inner nest of mothers? Let me face the cold, and develop hardness. I'm soft at my own peril. "Grow" means danger, risk-taking, possible self-destruction in the process. New selves will emerge—me, not my bodyguards, me, not my mollifiers, me, not lackeys and valets and apologists who "spare" me from outer trial. A new me. Forging another link, in evolution's internal little own private race, the evolving man, who comes against outer things and is knocked around and his senses rearranged.

I'm in the fore. I'm changing. The new me is emerging—someone else. Goodbye to me as known: you'll serve a use as a reference file, by which progress may be measured in that new person, who assumes my name, my surface identity, and a slice of the old reputation as a sop to tradition and a small concession-offering to "continuity," that strange time-personality myth. Now another person is completing this, this "confession," that an earlier hand had begun. This "other person" wants to have done with this writing to put the paper aside and have the *world* to grapple with—an outside-words world, where activity takes place. Papers are for recording and relating and concluding. From one word to the next old becomes new. I have a me to prove, untried yet.

A SMALL INTERIOR SEQUENCE, DESCRIBED

(Extended sub-title, with private plea to reader:)

*(It begins with a coincidence of my wanting to do what
I actually am doing. Then it goes on, and finally it ends.
Events eventually do, you know. Newer events come
along. In me all this takes place. Enough of this sub-title.
Now for the text. That's where this essay's substance ought
to be found. Read it through. When the words stop, stop.
The writer-reader partnership is essential. I need you.
Please need me, and leap from this sub-title to the text
itself. May its mere words confine much matter. And may
its manner much please. Skim gently, with your approving
eyes.)*

(The text itself, culminating the essay:)

When you find yourself doing something, and it dawns on you
that the thing you're doing is what you would *like* to be doing, and you realize that you're doing something that you *want*
to do—then it occurs to you that it's time to remind yourself
that you ought really to be pleased; it's the perfect opportunity
to be pleased: the conjunction of your doing something and
your *wanting* to do just that. So you *are* pleased. You're pleased
upon reflection, in an intellectual sort of way. Even emotionally, you're kind of pleased. Enjoy it quick. It's being consumed.
Soon, that rare conjunction has fled. Then you're your usual
miserable self. But *now*, realize you're happy! Hurry! It's dissolving already! The fortuitous combination is losing grip. Seize
the echo! Take mental cognizance! The emotions are untrust-
worthy. They lull us into complacency, where all seems right:
then customary suffering comes, worry, anxiety, dreary grim
depression. The latter is my now state.

Such is my moody process, from this essay's happy start to
this solemn end. I've returned to unhappiness, in its newest

version. I'll analyze it. In so doing, I'll break it apart. It'll be re-placed, by another compound feeling. That's my prospect. I'll know it, when I feel it. But not till. It's yet to be. Meanwhile, my current now is different from my previous now, I'll slightly examine it. *Close* inspection won't do. I'm afraid what I might find. I cautiously prod. The next now is being issued. I'm in it, already.

THE SOURCE OF CONSCIOUSNESS IS SOMETHING NEGATIVE WITH BEING?

Consciousness is the failure of being.

Self-consciousness is the mark of people with identity-problem.

Consciousness may not be the *failure* of being, but the *symptom* of being's lack of identity with itself.

When something is wrong, we think. Thinking implies trouble, problem.

What's wrong? *We* are.

We're wrong, therefore we think.

WHO AM I? ME OR ANOTHER? OR BOTH? THE URINE-ELIMINATION TEST MAY SIMPLIFY MY SELF-DOUBT.

I feel a signal—a message from my bladder—I must go to the bathroom.

But perhaps that signal or message was meant for someone else.

No, then it wouldn't have chosen *my* body to operate in.

If telephone lines can cross wires, so perhaps can nerves be transferred.

Well, I once phoned long-distance and reversed the charge. In *this* case, could I have received a long-distance call by, or on behalf of, the *caller* needing to go to the bathroom?

Possibly. It depends on the interchangeability between parts of people. You may be partner or proxy to someone else's part, which in *you* has become operative, though to *him* still belonging.

I'd like to get to the bottom of this.

So would he—or whoever it is. Have it out, with him.

What debate can there be, if he's not *here*?

He is—partly.

But intangibly. Or we overlap, or bisect, and all areas outside have turned invisible. I'm confused, for him. I'd like to be me—but he's in my place.

It's *your* territory—kick him out.

I got here first?

Sure—he's trespassing; keep him in his place,

But I'm not sure what *my* place is.

You'll know, once you eliminate him. For then only *you*'ll be left—in a clear landscape, rid of his obstruction.

I'll urinate first—to get him out of my system.

That's it—exorcise him.

(Returning from the bathroom:) Ah, now I feel like me again.

Good. When you're rid of your foreign bodies, things are much simpler—and you know who you are.

I do? Yes, I do.

Are you uncertain?

Not for a while. When I *am* again, I'll pour it out, I'll purge it, down the drain.

A good system, you have. Keep to your own water level. Don't clog your drain. When in doubt, overflow,

FINDING OUT WHO I AM

"You're exactly like so-and-so," someone told me. "Yeah, but that's where the resemblance ends," I qualified; and was told no more.

Then the other guy went away, and being now alone I wondered about so-and-so being too much like me—enough like me as to destroy me. Valuing myself, I was jealous of him.

So I determined to meet him, which never happened before, only I would make it happen now. So the guy who told me about so-and-so being like me—I went to that guy, and said, "Introduce us."

"Sure," he said, "you'll really recognize him," smiling. That scared me. My existence was threatened.

So the introduction was arranged, like I had asked. I was brought before so-and-so, and was left with him, for our go-between "beat a hasty retreat," as someone once invented.

Face-to-face was I with so-and-so, and we traded eyes. I found him to be me. Thus disconcerted, we had to take a long trip, and started off together, by now inseparable companions.

After getting off the traveling vehicle and on and off another one, we walked deep into a crowded city, until exhaustion "overtook" us.

So we set our bags down and each lay down on his portable air mattress. But before sleep "overtook" me, I started up in worry, gripped in the bolt of a thought pierced through and through with anxiety.

It was this (under the stars of night): "what if I wake up tomorrow morning and can't find myself? Then where would I be?"

I tried to resolve these doubts through meditation, but failed. That's when I thought of a more *practical* solution.

And this is what it was: I would tie a banana peel to my ankle, so that when I would wake up, I would at once look to see whose ankle had the banana peel. And whoever that ankle belonged to, would be me. Then self-recognition would begin to dawn on me, through the process of identification; and securely I'd rest in what I was.

So I put this plan into action. I tied a banana peel too my ankle. (One, not the other.) Then I fell asleep.

Unknown to me, so-and-so woke up in the middle of the night and decided to rob me of certitude. Stealthily, he untied from my ankle the banana peel and instead tied it onto his own ankle. The prank being prepared, he delivered himself of a smirk (wasted on the night air, like a desert flower born to blush unseen), and fall back asleep.

I awoke before him in the morning. I felt lost.

To be found with reassurance, I looked around for that banana skin in which I had deposited, in repose, for safekeeping, my valued identity.

I saw it on sleeping so-and-so's ankle. I was taken in, deceived. For I considered him to be me.

So I *treated* him like me: my first obedience to the Golden Rule. He woke up, and disclaimed being me. To settle the dispute on amicable terms, I pointed to the telltale skin of banana still tied on to his ankle. (It took on the significance of Desdemona's lost handkerchief: but that's another story.)

So-and-so said no, he was he. I was me: evidence to the contrary, for he had "planted" it—just to upset or confuse me.

Ever since then, I've kept to myself. I don't know what's become of so-and-so. We parted company that instant, and that's been our state ever since—apart.

I'll ponder on *outward* things; but first, let me get out of the way this matter of who I am. If I'm not just another so-and-so, then wherein lies my distinction? How can I be told apart—and from whom?

I'll solve it soon. Give me time.

My progress is slower than time running out. My state will change. Will death complicate the difference?

Me. A most personal matter.

Me. So what of it?

I'm not just being another? I'm not just being kept in reserve, by another?

No. Surely, I am precisely what I am?

"That's far too simple," a voice delays. So I'm stuck. I don't know, and I fade.

STANDING ERECT ON NO PREMISE

My right shoe is on the wrong foot.

What foot is that?

The right foot.

But the right foot is the right foot for it. Where else would you put a right shoe?

On the wrong foot.

That's some feat, if you can do it.

It's a self-defeating feat?

Yes, you get off on the wrong foot.

You're too tight-laced.

Tongue-in-heel, my sole's to reveal.

I take all *walks* of life in my stride.

Then tread softly, for your mouth is foot-ridden.

So *runs* our day. On that stand, by twin props base me skyward, and I rise flat.

Your feet are in the clouds?

Yes. Grounded there.

WORN BY MAN IN THREE PARTS

Part One

I had to close up my foot to put my shoe on. But it opened up after the shoe was on. The shoe fell apart.

Moral: You can't cover up man's opening out at the bottom of things.

Part Two

I pulled my hand together to enclose it in a glove. But then the hand ran apart, and there was a *former* glove.

Moral: You've got to hand it to man: he'll always be bursting out.

Part Three

My head was meek and humble for the hat to fit. Then, all pride broke loose. From within, vanity split the hat, with its bulging mental biceps. The head poured out. The hat is flat and torn. Man had ripped its seams. Man is the head of what he wears, and wears it through—or wears through it; tearing, then discarding. Man comes first. What's put on is subject to coming off, gently or violently. Man rules. He won't be encumbered.

Moral: Extract it from textual body.

A COMPLAINT OF NOT BEING LIKE OTHERS

Such varieties of different people there are! Who am I not to include myself! But the others contrast strangely with me, despite an intriguing veil of similarities. May they suffer appetite, and rage unattainable desire, just as I? Have they my abyss of self-doubt, do they lack a confident appraisal of their abilities to combat the world? Then internally, where distinctions reign and unique qualities are developed, they might actually be compared with me! Unfavorably to me, or to them?, judgment might fairly pass, Am I their superior, because I personally exist inside my skin? The same measurement goes for *them*, too: and though one of them, I feel my isolation grow beyond endurance, as I hatefully am closed outside their intervening companionship and frantic rescue attempts. Alone, I dwell, and there is my salvation and my grace.

If men, surely they feel for women as I do? And when they eat, must hunger be appeased, as in my case? Most decidedly yes; as on the occasion when *their* sleepiness is rewarded with sleep, and mine finds the same peace, as though one formula binds us. And when they want money from the personal economy of need, isn't that my pattern also? Some of them may delight in reading a book, where this pleasure agrees mightily with *me*, linking us in lovely mental pursuit. But my differences are shocking, unless I lose pretense of myself and drop that arrogant pride so that, in close ranks, I may meet my brothers, and be enveloped within, among, according to, their principles I do not even feel. Insanely, revoltingly, I am *not* one of them! Though my blood warms to melt in compassion for all of us, plignt and a fate the same,

My fellow men! I condescend to be your inferior; and may your power be my trial! I am only me; but you, you are many; there is a standard and a norm among you, while for me abnormality is my only convention, to which traditionally I owe my freakiness. You are what you are, and I can't read your inner hesitation, But I'm not anything, being guided into active motor by an unspotted will that urges a split of impulse, forced into opposite motivations! I cringe, and can't move. But you *seem* to function, as only your apparent form dwells in my eye. I'm assailed by sickly incertitude, and deeply in trouble, the frail battlefield of unyielding instinct against my riotous inhibitions of experience: I've learned, through failure and defeat, to consciously unthrone myself of pure and direct action, fearing penalties I deserve or don't. What can I do, so afflicted, wrenched back from the simple paths that others *seem* to course, and of necessity share my impossibility to negotiate, as *their* substance turns from the same sickly clay? Only one thing I'm immune from: death; although the others are not prohibited, and may savour it nicely at the end. I'm satisfied, since immortality redeems me from their common lot, who die like flies. But immortality as I *am*? I'd rather die, to tell the truth,

My fellow men, make me one of you. Who am I to abstain? Claim me back, and let our wills blend. You'll find in me a brother, not reluctant, but consenting as you do to what conserves our unity and preserves our grave community from exemption or exception, I renounce myself, and am willing to join. Brothers, will you have me?

No? Then to hell with you, and I'm back to myself, which is my own proper loss and gain. It's what I possess, outstanding as my personality stands formed. Lonely yet? Well, I'll endure it, this time. Let them have themselves, and be many. I'll be few or nothing or one, as my creed and credo, and will independently have individual aims, the carbon duplicates of their own copy. But better, yet, for this quality: mine. Who else belongs to myself? Only I do. My loneliness is not the least bit crowded, I have lots of room, for industry and recreation, Let them be. Am I? Maybe, I'm what I have, if only I can take inventory. My business deserves standards, which my work will be to construct, Then I might seem normal to myself, and all others fall redundant, in their well-kept distances, to the natural artifice of integrity I prop myself into, feed from, contribute to: oh, what am I, after all?

THOUSANDS OF SELVES—IN CIVIL STRIFE, OR IN ALL-OUT UNITY? ALL ARE IN ME.

I have thousands of selves. Each one is selfish. Sometimes the selfishnesses of many of my selves are all pulling together in concert. That gives me extra power.

But when the selfishnesses of too many of my selves are opposing the selfishnesses of other selves, I'm torn apart by conflict. That's bad for me.

Or maybe is it good? Could be.

All my warring selves. Sometimes amassed in equal armies against each other; other ties consolidated into a complete unit to war against life's adversities, when, undivided, they're all needed, at full strength, to meet a crisis. They join ranks, eliminate warring functionalism, and become a mighty power bloc. Thousands of selves, all for me! Who am I?

BY YOUR APPEARING I GET MY ALLOTTED QUOTA OF YOUR MYSTERY-BULGING BEING

What are you in your being? My only way of telling is by how you seem. So I study all the ways that you appear. Sometimes you appear something far behind in time what presently you're being. You may be even feeling what's also behind in time what you're being. Possibly you appear to be something of a more remote-in-time being than the being which you're less belatedly feeling. But even what you feel may be slightly out of date compared with the fresh being that's always emerging from you.

I'm annoyed to be limited to only the avenue of how you seem, as my only accessible avenue toward the estimation or approximation of your dear but—or dear therefore—or dear because—hard-to-approach being. To me, all I get of you is via the rays of your seeming. I'd wish to have more direct access, but such a wish may be to beg the issue with the impossible.

There you are. Between you and me lies your seeming. Can I embrace and make contact with your seeming? Does therein lie sufficient of your being? Or is all your being wrapped up in, and constituted by, your seeming? Shall I be content to equate the seeming I have with the being you are?

Or is your being *fully* your seeming? Is it as simple as that?—the two making one?

Your being comes to me by appearing—and both comprise a mystery.

If you stop remaining the mystery, then your being stops mattering to me, and your appearing shines unneeded.

Who are you? How, by what, are you? It's written in appearance's language—but especially for me.

HE

Did you ever meet my friend Charles?

That reminds me of an interesting story.

But never mind. Some other time.

But to get back to my original point.

If you ever met him, you'd know just what I mean.

The Charlesness of him. Pure Charlesness, and nothing else.

Which brings to mind several interesting comparisons.

And how they multiply! A thousand people immediately flock to mind.

How prolific of you, Charles.

HOOKING UP ON SOMEONE ELSE'S HEARING

Was that you I heard playing the drum before?

No, I was listening—you heard me listening.

You mean sounds came out of your listening?

No, *into* it; but you *shared* my listening.

I heard you hear the drums?

Yes, via indirect experience.

But why can't I hear my *own* sounds?

What I hear *become* your own sounds.

Then I'm too dependent on you.

No, when I'm not hearing anything, you can go to work on the *memory* of all my past sounds.

Is that an endless supply? Are they all happy sounds?

No, so select the best and savor them. Tune in; (on both my ear channels) monitor and moderate all that stirs there, from my audible lifetime so far.

SOMEONE IS HEARING ME LISTENING! I HOPE WHAT PASSES THROUGH MY EARS SOUNDS ALL RIGHT TO HIM. I'M CONDUCTING A SPECIAL FILTERING OF THE ORIGINAL MUSIC; REFINING IT, AS THE AGENT OF ITS ULTIMATE RECEIVER: WHO'LL HEAR IT MORE IDEAL THAN *I'M* GETTING IT!

I heard a noise from the other room. It came from the room *you* were in. It was the noise of a few instrumental musicians. The drums had a special beat. Was that *you* I was hearing playing the drums?

No, I had no instrument, so you heard me *listening* to them.

Oh. Well, you were listening very loud.

Sorry. Next time I'll tone down my listening, before transferring it to you.

Thanks. My hearing is so acute, it pains me to hear a false note, or a too-high volume. The reason I have good taste is to balance my nerves. It defends me against offensive extremes from a screaming environment. Sensitivity means pain-potential. So I'm dependent on your good help. Not that I want the blunting or the dulling of the sound waves; but sounds of harmony, not discordant noise. My conditions are delicate, and so I seem extra demanding. But pleasure can so often be a matter of scruples, inches away from genuine displeasure, or an octave degree in terms of sound. I hope my "preciousness" doesn't annoy you?

Next time, if the musicians play too loud, I'll hear it softer, so that, through me, your nerves can be quietly appeased. I'll pass it on somewhat muted. Through earsay, you'll belatedly and ideally hear. I'm glad to be your filter.

Thanks for your intervening and editorializing conduction for my benefit. I'm already soothed.

TO APPEAR BETTER THAN TO BE

How's your etiquette?
Mannered, but serviceable.
In what guise are you well-presented?
Of appearing better than I only am.
Does hypocrisy erase its trace?
I seem *naturally* right, *simply* good.
What worth does you pretense affect?
Infallibility's high merit.
Does you deception always work?
Intelligence can detect it out.

THE "NOT-THERE MAN," AND THE TROUBLE WE TAKE IN FAILING FULLY EVER TO FIGURE HIM OUT.

He's the "not-there man," even though I just saw him all weekend. We saw him at breakfast, lunch, dinner, for three days, and sometimes between those meals, at times before or after them; all the more, then, was that impression driven home, of what he was: the "not-there man." His body and his face were there, his clothes and shoes, his hair and his smile, his hands and his walk, and what he did: such as, he helped prepare us good meals, and he himself was the most prominent eater of them. How, then, with all this, with his very firm presence—his solid form—was he, for us—the "not-there man?"

By his absence from what we were saying. He seemed not to look at us when we were saying anything. Or he looked only in the way of waiting for us to finish; politely and patiently asking—or seeming to—"When are you going to stop talking, how long must I wait?" He wasn't angry, he was smiling and polite—was he seething, covertly? He had an amiable, unvarying, quite friendly, and sweetly bred smile. Yet he was waiting for us to finish talking even as we just *began* trying to make our points.

I therefore accuse him of lack of interest. That's the main conclusion I now draw, from his behavior with us. Somewhere, he was abstracted, while being with us. He just—"wasn't there."

What was pulling him always away from us? What spell was he under? What fascination drew him away? Was he absorbed in a serial daydream? Was he compounding some mathematical formula that was the grand solution, the key on a master scale, to thousands of lesser mathematical problems ever since men first started to count? Was he composing the first, last, and only silent opera that would completely satisfy the most vocally vain of all soloists?

Was he secretly painting, without benefit of brushwork, the first purely perfect invisible painting? So complete, it needed absolutely no frame—for what would profane it? And the banality of it being *hung*—never! Yet was he doing the mental brushstrokes on it, continuously?

Or was he, infinitely within, carving, non-word by non-word, the greatest non-verbal poem that ever did not and will never exist?

Or maybe, simply, there was nothing there at all: a nothing that totally abstracted him. Was he contemplating his own internal emptiness? Was he surrendering his full non-consciousness to a positively unpositive vacuum?

Or was he haunted by a trite, childish ghost tale? Or was he plunging through the innermost layers of an undefinable neurosis? Or was he just remembering something? Or was he trying to forget something? Or was he concentrating on a mystical line of steady nonsense? Was he exploring God's dimensions? Was he inventing a new religion? Or paganizing an old one? Or solving the riddle of how to reconcile individuals versus mass society? Or was he trying to breathe reviving life into an extinct old species of mammal, fish, or insect? Or was he remembering an old love? Or was he *wondering* about something?

Those are possibilities. But he was inaccessible, so nothing is proven; nor was there even the confirmation of a clue. He was a blank, and there was no puzzling him out. Easier is it to find the source of thought in a nearly dead fish.

Maybe he was just plain dumb? Yet he was college-educated, and held down a responsible career in a fund-raising branch of non-profit industry. Employees under him took his orders. And he had a bright wife, and two lively teen-age daughters by a former but now divorced wife.

Anyway, what was in his head? Why didn't he at least heed us when we spoke? Was anger preventing him? But why would he have been angry? We were good guests, we never offended him. We courteously obeyed his house-rules.

Was he just blissfully happy, and drawn to the core of that happiness? Or so depressed, he could only smile with the meek blandness of an amiable deaf person when other people shout in vain to be heard?

He was guilty of a failure to communicate. Or were *we* the guilty ones? We were not getting across. We were not getting through. We brought up subject after subject. We expounded, elaborated, were engaging and witty. We were informative, we were educated, articulate, of verbal and conversational sophistication.

Yet, to us, he remained the "not-there man." Where was he? Should we be offended? Should he be offended? *Was* he offended?

Maybe his wife would know. We asked her. She ambiguously defended him without implicating us in any crime whatever.

We enjoyed the food, the country scenery, the lovely interior and fine bedrooms, all niceties like that. But our host—the "not-there man"—why was he just not there?—except only by his presence?

He was definitely present. Yes, but not accounted for.

Inscrutable, or enigmatic, like fascinating women, or intriguing continentals, or semi-westernizing orientals.

The "not-there man:" we were interested in him, and not in anyone else—the each-other guests, or his wife and family.

He ate robustly. He *seemed* to listen when we spoke. He even answered: but from—in the context of relevance we were always initiating—some uncanny vacuum. Was he filled with a *profound* emptiness? Was he too deep, to reply?

We're all back in the city. I'll invite him to dinner, and try again. We'll probe him, in *our* territories. Grounds for some insight, at least?

I just want to put him on the map. To locate, define, slot him. I'm intrigued, but also angry. He's putting me through this obsessive bother. I *am* obsessed. I'm the maniac, *he*'s my subject.

I want to *found* him. I want him to "be-there." *Some*where, where he *is*. To penetrate him—*within*. To cast in him a world. To finally "world-him-out." To get him—*out-here*.

Into the light of daylight. Who is he? *Who*, not what?

If I knew that . . . Well, he's invited for dinner: he and his wife. Let's see, now.

Yes, let's just see. *Him*. To see the inner him. To un-"not-there" him, as, finally, a found man.

HOW I FEEL, HOW I SEEM, HOW I RELATE

Feeling is how our being appears to us.

Seeming is how our being appears to another.

The other induces our feeling from our seeming—often inaccurately. And he can't *feel* our feeling. Only *we* can feel our feeling.

When we *feel* our being, we *imagine* how we seem to another—often inaccurately. And we can't really feel *his* feeling that *he* gets from our seeming. All we can feel is our feeling.

But bridges are extended, via compassion, Sympathy, empathy, "reading in," identification with the other: to various degrees of accuracy, symbolically, the interpenetration by one level or plane of another. To the degrees of these overlappings, there are fellow-feelings, "feelings-for;" and we're thereby less alone, but involved with others; less in isolation: but partaking in others' lives, with imaginative penetration, with more or less degree of accuracy.

Summary or conclusion aftermath:

My being communicates itself to me by how I feel.

My being communicates itself to another by how I seem.

But we project and relate—the other and I.

THE HUMAN SELFSAME TALKING LISTENER

The loquacious talker paused to make a point. (He had already made so many. What! Yet another?)

Upon the point where his pause was, he stopped or started, finished and began, so that more points were meanwhile getting made, but were lost to further points that superseded the earlier ones. Meanwhile, he was getting across other points, but hesitated and tried to retrace his verbal steps to finish up an earlier point he had been making, or merely to get back to it. In thus reversing his gears, however, he found himself quite lost. So he appealed to his listeners: "Where was I?" They weren't a bit of help. There was no reference index for distinguishing prior points and picking out approximate categories. So the talker was bogged down in the labyrinth of successiveness he had unstintingly woven.

"You digressed from your own digressions," a listener criticized. The talker admitted how only too true that was. But he recovered sufficiently to forge forward, like life and time, with some utterly new points. Nature may forget a hash made of something, and start all over from virgin scratch. Not quite. It goes according to prior models, which in grim succession evolve, or in some cases fall flat extinct. Nature is prodigious, in endless fertility, from inexhaustible resources, ever freshly inventive, adaptive, innovational, improvisational, impulsive, with random abandon.

So was the talker, who went on, clearing up and gathering together new points, in passing. His listeners really did listen. Could they never get enough of him? No; they were his listeners.

Though critical, some of them were, as listeners. But that's part of listening well. Ever listening, to keep up with the ever talking. The talking never wound down, nor did the listening. It was an equal but opposite competition, in feats of endurance, prodigies of stamina, deterrents to exhaustion, hardy withstanders of fatigue'e enormous buildup. But the fatigue never dared intrude. The listening, the talking, the points, went swollen through a trail of digressions branching out from earlier ones. Is not every event a renewed digression? Disconti-nuity is constantly emerging. What it's discontinuous from, are its oddly sorted predecessors. Renewal starts all over. We pick up, and leave off. There's simultaneity, of points unrelated save by time's coincidence. We can never catch up with it all.

Listeners die, talkers die, but points get made from new mouths to new ears. People are born, for this "purpose." Mat-ter gets communicated, as pollen gets passed from flower to flower by dying bees along the way. The bearers of content are the talkers, to the listeners. Listeners turn talkers, in their turn. Lots get said. The said that gets heard. And repeated distort-edly, with new matter added. The words that go around. The words that fill the air. The buzzing air, the vocables that hum. Impressed in, on the brainy ear. The points that cross and criss. Divergent semi-points, from major branches. The collective sounds that go around. The loud and soft ones. The pauses, the resumptions. Continuity's context of discontinuities. Waves of intelligence, booming in the lower air. A network of human meaning. For little ears, along the way; in a round of relays. For mental devouring. Soft and loud, a concert.

We're born and caught and pass into this. Proverbs and old saws, wise homilies, the inbred traditions, the verbal constructs, the artifice of our language, a laying together of tongues, on a multiple ear's tuning fork. Yes, we get the mes-sage: of a great many points. Points past pointing out. The pouring out, point past point, of digressions that converge to-ward central meanings: and then fork out again, like delivery trucks from a newspaper building. Our air is wave-filled. We're congested, in meaning's garden. All these words, to arrive and depart. Summing what? They divide, rather, in multiple ways. The daisy chain of meanings, to link us. And we're spun along, on such beads. And so we find points, to discuss: cells of our collective talk. Or are we one talker, and the same listener: all embodied, by one huge person, whose cells change in history?

Is the human race a person and himself, talking and listening? Era by era, altering the complex points? And being altered, by the points, slowly evolving. The person is new, each time. Listening and speaking, points replace points. Ever the latest news is on his tongue. At the ears, interpretation forms. Thus he instructs and amuses himself, with information and analysis and playful parodies upon all that, in the passage of human material, on a slow safari through time: while sitting down. Talking late. An endless issuing forth of ideas. Keeping the body and soul intact, of the one living mind, in which ideas and individuals, in passing, partake. To build up what structure? Our high monument, to what?

I DISLIKE THE EASY GROUP LIKING OF HARRY. THERE'S MORE LIFE ON THE SIDE OF *DISLIKING* HIM. WITH THIS ORIGINALITY, I'LL OVERTHROW THE PEOPLE-BLOB OF HARRY-LIKING.

We all like Harry, and that makes him so popular. Or do we like him *because* he's so popular? Now I'm questioning whether I *do* like him. I decide not to. No, he's very dislikable. That's because the liking of him has been made stale and flabby and overgeneralized (thus devitalized) by the unquestioning consensus of the people who go along with the overall drift of all the others in readily liking Harry as a herd act. No, I'll pull out. I'll dissent. I'll take a more original, but unpopular, standpoint. That will pour some fresh water or fresh air onto this dusty, too-long-settled matter. I'll inject some life into this so-sterile issue—or non-issue, as it were. I hope Harry doesn't mind. He's basking with fat-cat complacency in being liked by mass conformity. He's enamored with the numbers of it all, rather than the individual quality of each person's liking him—there is no individual quality: he's liked in a blur or blend of people agreeing with their own group abstraction. But quantitatively, Harry is flattered by all that. He'll become a Buddha-like idol, at this rate of trend, projecting the tendency in a span of unreflective time. He'll rule, and why not? Power is pleasant, if you can have it. I object. I hate his being liked so indiscriminately. I'll start a counter-trend. I'll rip him off his perch, in the sweet reversal of time. I'll unHarry him, of all that thoughtless adulation.

THE MOTH AND THE CATS
(ALTERNATE TITLE: THE CATS AND THE MOTH)

Two cats who lived in someone's apartment saw a moth fluttering open-winged around, because it was spring hot weather
and the window had been opened.

The cats wanted to kill the moth, if at all possible. So they
studied it steadily, with big predatory eyes, eyeing their chosen
prey, all tensely alert to spring at it when opportunity turned
practical and the occasion was ripe for the kill. The cats were
only beasts, after all. Their "morality" had strictly jungle origins, and their origins were still there in action, whether that
action was latent, potential, dormant, or imminent—or actually
active. In fact, morality was furthest from the cats' two minds.

The moth was fluttering up the wall, with open wings. The
moment was approaching, when one or both of the hunters
would poise, spring, leap, claw, and seize. The moth didn't have
the pale ghost of a chance. In fact, it quite resembled a pale
ghost, but haunted rather than haunting.

There were lots of varying-height objects, strewn all about
the "Victorian" apartment, for the cats to jump to and from, in
angling in on their prey, stalking it up and down and here and
there, setting up, perched, poised for the strike. Altogether, the
odds were greatly in favor (though no human gamblers were
present) of the cats' conquest of the helpless, harmless moth.
This conquest would mean death, to the little latter.

Then the cats couldn't find it. They looked for hours. Yet
it was in open view. Sometimes just quarter of an inch away,
when inadvertently the cats drew close. But the cats had no clue.
Altogether, the "scent" was lost.

The moth was masterfully self-protective. It had folded up
its fluttering wings, like a gentleman folding up his umbrella,
and was still, white and still, on the similarly white wall, fac-

ing the wall, motionless for dear life, exuding no odor, no cat-palpable trait by which to be fatally detected.

The cats, plainly, were puzzled. Perplexed. Totally confounded. Bewildered. They looked and scratched and searched, but could find—nary a clue.

The moth survived. By becoming inconspicuous, drawing no attention. It's *still* facing the wall, with wings folded in. It takes no chances. It defended itself inactively.

The cats, of course, survived as well. They got regularly fed by their mistress, with real cat-food—not mothy found improvisations. So they didn't *need* the moth, to keep life and limb together, for filling their already pampered stomachs.

The cats soon forgot their failure. They were stupidly resilient, and attended to other matters.

The moth is still there, on the wall: wings infolded, in symmetrical stillness, a vertical inanimate rectangle in slight appearance. Facing the wall. The back to the former danger. Ignored, even forgotten, never recognized, by those stupid dumb beasts.

I'm neither stupid, dumb, nor a beast. I witness it all. In imagination, not in the apartment. I live and think about them. All they do, those three, is live. That suffices *them*. But not me, for I'm superior.

TO WORRY? OR NOT?

Mark posted a letter in the mail box. He had stamped, addressed, and sealed the envelope. Before that, he had folded the letter (after writing it) and inserted it in the aforesaid envelope. The postage amount was correct, the address had been carefully checked; the letter would reach its destination tomorrow; yet would it? He worried. Maybe the post office personnel had a conspiracy against him. But it's paranoiac to think that way. Yet he *was* thinking that way. Then he was paranoiac? How *could* he be? He was *Mark*. And Mark didn't see himself as paranoiac. So trust the post office. So he did, and stopped worrying.

The next day he got a phone call in reply to that letter, which had just been received. Thus he learned to trust trust. Trust had been found trustworthy: *this* time, anyway.

(A non-trivial title:)

IDEAS ARE MENTAL VERSIONS OF THE OUTER
WORLD. THE WORLD IS AN ELABORATE IDEA. IT'S
FORMED TO OUR THRUSTING MIND. WE HUMANIZE
OVER ITS CHAOS. WE ADJUST OUR CHANGES TO ITS.
EACH LIFE ILLUSTRATES THIS NON-DUALISM: THE
WORLD IN THE HEAD, OF THE HEAD, BY THE HEAD:
WE ARE THE WHAT OF WHAT WE SEE. THOUGHT
IS THERE, ALL MATTERED OVER. FOR WE ARE THE
WORLD CONCEIVED: EACH ONE REVEALS IT; HIS
OWN WAY.

It's dark. Is the world still there?

Sure. Don't you believe in the unseen?

Yes, but only by an act of faith. In the *easy* sense, seeing is be-lieving.

But some of the most valuable ideas come from difficulty.

Is conceiving the unseen more valuable than seeing what's vis-ible?

Sometimes. Enough so that the effort is often worth making.

I can't *see* your point, but I'll take your *word* for it.

You'll take it on trust?

What else? There's no concrete evidence. I'll *assume*.

Good. While it's still dark. Ideas play freely, when objects ap-pear absent. For ideas stand us in their stead. They'll do, as sym-bolic things themselves.

That's sneaky of ideas. Like rats, they play when the real cats are away.

Without ideas, what are merely things? For ideas don't just fill up the black night; they define the real toys of day, assign-ing names, properties, and identifications to those unformed clusters. Ideas make events solid. They select concreteness, and show how. They reveal the actual. They register change.

They reckon, given what's been. They anticipate by computing. They're journalistic historians, on the running flow of Now.

But ideas aren't the objects themselves?

They're *about*. Thus, by mentality's means, we take digestible chunks of worldly proliferated matter. We then impose sense. And take control, in effect.

Does the world mind?

It's flattered, that man takes such a vivid interest, however selective, in its wildly disconnected events. Man roughly puts them in shape, in an idea form. Ideas thus domesticate the unruly motions of matter. We've manicured, harnessed, and tamed a whole irrational jungle, and civilized the heart of chaos. Our mental realm, now, is the official world: subject to constant alterations, of course, for new evidence pours in, to contradict the old. Made mental, with the man-made stamp on it. Finally, our ideas have constituted what's universal. We've tricked the world, and snapped our trap shut, on our now captive animal. It's now our household pet—the formerly old bad world. It serves us. But it snaps back, and bites. We had better beware.

THE WORLD'S INSUFFICIENCY MAKES MIRACLES NEEDED, GIVES EMPLOYMENT TO DREAMS, PROVOKES IMAGININGS. THE WORLD CALMLY IGNORES THEM. WHAT INCOMPATIBLES!

I was told it's a waste of time to make up miracles. But I have to do it, to make up for the world being so imperfect. But who am I, so stuck-up as to consider this fine world imperfect?! Maybe so, but it's impossible to accept it as it is—it's way off center, leaves a huge imbalance in the gap: growing a need for miracles in my world-perfecting mind. In the end, the mind judges: the world is the judged. The judge, in rendering verdict, redistributes justice to fair out the odds and restore harmony to the semblance. The mind redoes; the world lacking, or the world having overplus of the wrong. Ideals cure this, for the mind. The world is too chronic, incorrigible, to take the cure: the *mind* must take it, for it. The mind miraculously retouches a plain canvas that was painted to chance. The mind unchances it—setting up seeming control: till the world unseats this interloper, shakes it off, and is unsaddled of its mentalizer—to gallop off, on its riderless random.

I hang on. I dream away. Yet a billion years of specialized dreaming couldn't purge the world of itself. The failure of miracle to change the unchangeable—except by delusion, illusion, hallucinating. Reality tampered with—humoring the tamperer.

Needing such touchings-up, manicuring, making cosmetic, such undisordering, of a world, to bear it: my mind is suffered by the world to grandly curb, fuss, fiddle, set right, overrule. But my restless material, when disturbed too far, or hemmed unnaturally in, slips off my hold, and unweaves my meddling fabric. My dream is disassembled; to reorganize, along lines meeting with more docility from the implacable world.

Reality refractory in tailoring itself to my dreams, I look for stuff more lenient, though synthetic, to my dream's specifications. An uncooperating world withholds its grim permission. I'll have to seize what I can, being barred a license. My heart will remake this sorry scheme of things entire, remold it to the heart's desire. And what *is* the heart's desire? Not known but felt. To make and not imitate. Purge dreams of the world, to let purity gather there where dreams originate. Let the *dreams* be standard: and the *world* fail, for not measuring up.

HOW, BY PAUSING IN TELLING SOMETHING, TO GIVE THE WHOLE SCENE SUCH EXTENSION THAT DURATION IS SURPASSED.

Delp was telling a story for all and sundry. On a glorious Sunday.

It was in a park expressly picked for picnics. The listeners were spread out on the earth's grassy cushion. Delp couldn't help looking at the weather: which stood itself in deep accord with the season most appropriate to it. And what did the *season* do? What was only logical: the season had related itself to its climate, and by that method was abiding in harmony with the continental location. Thus, atmospherically, all was well.

The picnic was being munched, edibly; for the occasion had been provided with food. Delp went on relating his narrative. His listeners were mostly girls who were sprawling. The boys were up playing ball, to work off some of their intensive young male energy. What more natural thing could be expected of them?—to keep their public virtue in check. The more the girls sprawled, the swifter and higher flew the boy's boisterous ball.

Delp's story seeped slowly into the afternoon. The gorgeous April sun seemed just made for that comfortable Western Hemisphere. Delp had no choice but to continue.

And the girls didn't break their stride, their listening stride, indolent outstretching, rather sensual. From time to time, Delp experienced a thrill.

And the boys' ball went higher; and in perfect safety, for there were no clouds to break. Heaven had assured a clarity of absolute azure. A choicest rejoicing rang round the clamoring picnic. Still, Delp lisped out his lengthy narrative. The syllables spilled their string of unbroken vowels upon the circle of lovelies. The girls' legs were skirting the issue. The afternoon sun could peek through.

Delp went on. The boys ranged their game farther away, along the shadows that fell lengthwise against the earth's shattering boundary. Their yells grew distant.

Abruptly, Delp paused in his story. Simultaneously, the listening of the girls had to pause, belonging to Delp's very process,

His story was not true, therefore interesting. When the season changed, and the girls grew up, and the boys were all working men, Delp stuck to his place, same as before. Loyalty means passing time's test, despite insurmountable difficulties. The picnic park was now a huge block of apartment dwellings, monotonously looking the same. The sun was blocked out, and the climate made no difference. Delp was squeezed in an alleyway, between two staggering buildings. His tongue was stilled. He was there, committed to memory. A former glorious occasion, of his holding forth ideally to the best audience, vanquishing his youthful rivals who were relegated to an athletic horizon, came clearly back, and made Delp stay there to keep his body sentinel over that which exalted all worth. Poor Delp was totally alone. But how beyond exactness itself was the recall of perfection! This was his controllable mastery. His untrue story had interested a lying-down audience, in a relaxed atmosphere of erotic tension. It was Delp's high spot. It clung to him at all times. To it, all other things stood sacrificed. That's to impart to life its most selected value in the mind's dominion over time. The joy it once conferred stuck perpetually to its place. Delp had never concluded his story. Thus on one unconcluded end, it could soar forever.

IF WHAT'S WRITTEN BECOME TRUE. IF WHAT'S
THOUGHT BECOMES TRUE. IF WHAT'S TRUE AC-
CUSES THE WRITER OF IT, OR THE THINKER OF
IT. DOES REALITY HOLD ITS MAKERS ACCOUNT-
ABLE? PATERNAL RESPONSIBILITY. CREATIVE
CONSEQUENCES. THE OPEN AUTHOR, OR THE PRI-
VATE COVERT THINKER. WORDS WRITTEN, VER-
SUS THOUGHTS THOUGHT, VERSUS WHAT'S MERELY
GIVEN. THE WORLD, AS THE SUM OF ALL TRUTH.

Whatever you write down becomes true . . .

That's too grave a responsibility. I refuse to write, in that case,
for I refuse to be burdened with the solemn, dire weight of the
true, if I've authored it.

But sometimes "true" is gay and light.

Still, truth is grim, It seems gospel-like, death-deep, majesteri-
ally grave, judicially stern, too strict and austere. Reality relies
entirely on "the true." The universe is decked out in "the true,"
and based inwardly on it in substance extrinsic, essence intrinsic. The truth is so real, I'd rather it be *given* me. To invent it is
too scary an act of creation. Let me *find* the real, as *there*. God
made it and said it. Let me just live it.

Then don't write.

I've already stopped writing. I'll take no chances that what I
write might become true.

However, what you *think* becomes true.

Oh, I don't mind that. It's not being responsible as if what I
wrote became true. Writing is an outward act, for the world
to detect. Thought, at least, can remain private. So let what I
think become true. It's an awesome act of control, and dear to
the fantasy of wish. But I won't be held accountable for it. Society won't suspect. Society examines what people write for evi-

dence of being authoritarian. The writer is accused, by the very reality he's stated. What's real would come back to haunt me if I wrote it. Paternity suits would be pressed upon me. Whereas the true that I think can't trace its origin to me, for at the source the evidence is destroyed, by the presence of later thought that covers over the earlier ones. I think, and go free—unharmed by all the truth my thought has made. Such truths are only orphans, and legally they have no right to my support. They float free. I do, too. The true, liberated from my fathering thought, releases my thought from the fathering of it. The world would never know. Such secrets are born, that investigation would never unearth. Whatever's true, was first thought by me. Let this truth take on its bodies, and grow out palpable. They were manufactured in hiding. They're part of the world. I find them, and claim surprise. I passively receive them. My children are unacknowledged.

(The essay's post-title:)

Preferring the truth given, rather than made by what I write. I can *think* truths into invention, but have no creator's responsibility for them the way I would if I wrote them into being. Writing is accountable for. A thought secretes out the truth, which joins the world as part of it, but the father mind is all a kept secret. Words betray the source of what truth they reveal. But a *thought* that makes a truth can sever forces with that made truth, and return unfound. Reality is a grim burden. Secrete it privately, then.

MYSTERY'S HEART OF KNOWLEDGE

I forgot to remember the future, so, until it comes, I remain
blank about it, although rather fearful and at the same time
hopeful. Even if I forget to wait, it reminds me by coming, and
so shocks me with wonder that I say, as though caught by surprise: "I knew you all along: you only come to verify me, confirm what I predict and prove the very living thing of what I
anticipate. I'm your master, once I'm certain of your arrival."

Then, to affirm my point, I emphatically resort to silence,
which, with a vacuum all around it, protects my inner superiority. It's amazing what pride will do, when cornered by forces
exerting physical pressure in the mystical expression of the
unknown. I'm very keen about the unknown, it's one of my
strongest points. I'm its major spokesman, and, when aroused
to eloquence, brilliantly keep my mouth shut and say positively
nothing, a little dogmatically, I think.

When I graduate from the unknown, my mind will abruptly
make contact with death, and communicate this chemical reaction to the cells, until belief overwhelms my body, negation
triumphs, and despair concludes what had been the history of
my emotions. Thus will I be illuminated, and with my mind
closed, the truth will face it. Truth is shy, you see, and evades
the living. Having commerce with the dead, hesitant truth becomes bold again, and shines: radiates, I think. Like a keen sun,
which, looked at from a certain angle, hides itself until the moment of blindness, and then appears. King Truth, reigning ab-
sently ever the living, an empire of subjects forbidden to see
it, but present in court and throne revealed before the dead,
hideous in the strange glory that the living would have loved to
know, but hated to see, governed by the futility of their gossip-
informative senses, the vanity of ego's pain and the self's personal pleasure.

I "BECAME" TRUTH; BUT LOST MYSELF. IT DEVOURED ME. I'M PART OF TRUTH; BUT AS A PERSON, UNKNOWN.

It was amazing what happened to me. Also so dangerous!

On a sudden, everything I said was true. I had become the living voice of truth. A responsibility so terrifying, it made me humbly humane. When you *have* the truth, all boasting converts to modesty.

And the power it gave me! I was now an oracle. People sought me out, perked up when I spoke. I was the voice of authority, which is what truth commands.

The least word I dropped, however obliquely casual, caused cataclysms of conscientious attentiveness.

It seems that the truth *adhered* to me, my voice ministering to it. I was the walking embodiment of it. I *was* truth.

That's quite a thing to be, truth. It's different, let's say, than being beauty, or virtue. Or evil, or poetry. Or lust, or even humanity. Or avarice, or any other walking thing. Or envy, or ignorance. Being truth: that's *really* something.

People flocked around me, in awe. I was accuracy's soothsayer. I turned out correct, every time. I was hardly me any more, I was so full of truth.

People wanted my predictions. I said no, the *future* wasn't mine, just the present, just the past. They went away disappointed.

I let them down; well, too bad. I didn't want to *commercialize* myself.

I just wanted to be, directly, what I was: simply, the *truth*.

But there were complications. How could I avoid them?: for what's so complicates, as truth?—especially, *being* it.

For one thing, as a matter of identity: was I *realistic* truth, or *imagination* truth? Or was I a bit of both? On was I *all* of both? And *more*, beside? Was I *every* truth, altogether, whatever their categories? Where did *my* province fall? What were the confines, if any, to my dominion's boundaries, in all extensions? I was unfathomable, if truth. There was *no* limit to me. Who can put a limit on truth? My depth couldn't be fathomed. My dimensions—uncharted. I went outside the world, I was metaphysics as well. Truth is boundless. Boy, did that increase me!

It's a load of trouble, too. Let me tell you.

I ceased being human altogether. I was no longer a person. I had become an abstraction.

Truth is *based* on humanity: humans are its medium, convey it to light. But I stepped over too far, lost myself, as truth took over.

I wanted my manhood back, in its frail but living status.

Too late. Emotions were forbidden; and no more self-interest. Truth had to insist on its neutrality: and eliminated me.

I was a would-be security risk, in truth's citadel. I was stripped of being. For safety, truth keeps its distance. From humans, for whom truth exists.

The end of me. My personal loss of identity is only a normal day in truth's endless reign.

An honor to be chosen for the sacrifice. A noble loss of self—in the truest cause.

But I'm unsung, to my dying glory. The cost of my small contribution is to stop being as me. My ego's role has died. Truth has no ego. Its mighty form has unseen edges. Its restless center pauses anywhere—to nourish on a blood sacrifice. More people are born. Truth need never starve. I'm replaced as an identity. Somewhere.

IN DEFENSE OF IGNORANCE

It's immoral to let one thing lead to another. But to prevent it would reverse logic, constituting an even dirtier sin. Science is plainly no good, since most of its facts are unwanted. "Phenomena" is one big crime; and blessed are the innocent, who forget. I'm against memory, which repeats in mind what occurred but should never have been.

Therefore each day I cultivate my ignorance, and develop a clarity of blankness within a brain that frustrates all knowledge, so purely self-sufficient and arrogant, almost dogmatic, it is on behalf of its own emptiness. This has destroyed my memory, for lack of nourishment; and I reign, supremely innocent.

When I smile, it's never cynical; it's simply a reflex, a dumb act of communication, revealing my stupidity in its simplest form, deepened by the inspiration of intensity. This is why my smile is so natural, free from the clever man's guilt: affectation.

So when I lie, I will be basically unchanged, and merely revert back to norm: the usual, as usual.

Perhaps already I'm dead? But I don't want to know. Knowledge would spoil me, and decay the corpse: against the smell of which, I've developed a cold in advance, reducing my senses clear of the unessential, which, superfluously, is everything contained within the outside of my ignorance. Thus I maintain myself, existing, living free of function, in a world completely dark, blackened even further by my blindness. I think this is quite an achievement, and ought to be the subject of a novel, based, first, on what must properly be called my autobiography. For I believe that words consolidate ignorance, and confirm the tedious but resolute path into the unknown, preserving emptiness and elevating the mind into a higher brainlessness, which no emotion or idea can penetrate, though disguised as primitive impulse and the will released by automatic instinct. There's just nothing I know; thus my void is perfect,

A DIALOGUE BY TWO MEN, ENDING IN A TALK ABOUT MAN. IT TAKES ALL OF MEN, TO MAKE THE ABSTRACTION, MAN.

How's your dignity?

It's not working. I forgot to wind it up.

How's your clock?

Full of pride and honor.

How's your reputation?

Lower than ever. I project an unfavorable image, so please remind me to change my publicity agent,

What's wrong with him?

That he couldn't disguise what's wrong with me.

What accuracy! He should have been a journalist.

But what an unfavorable impression of the world his reporting would create!

That's representing the world ungarnished, in its unmitigated truth.

How insulting the truth can be!

Yes, I hate when an insult is made righteous by honesty.

Honesty only *justifies* an insult.

Can honesty bear that much weight?

Yes, for reality reinforces it.

Can't they ever make themselves pleasant?

No, for that would falsely record the world.

Can't the world improve itself?

No, for it would deprive man of his tragedy.

What's so good about a tragedy?

It confers honesty and dignity. Pride is based on it.

Are they then tragically necessary?

Yes, the comic fool that man is.

Why comic, if tragic?

He's everything we know. Whatever *he*'s not, we don't know of. Whatever exists, *he* is. It all falls to him, first.

TRUTH UNSAID JUST ISN'T SO

Imagination is the world slightly expanded.

Really?

Of course.

Why "of course?"

Because I said so. Saying makes the thing said "so."

You don't say! You old so-and-so! "Imagination is the world slightly expanded." Is the corollary implied by that?

What corollary?

"The world is the imagination slightly shrunk."

Of course. Why not say it? It's true, isn't it?

Sure. Especially since you *said* it.

Good. If saying gives truth, there's much to be said.

If there's much to be said, there's much to be true.

Would a truth exist if it's unsaid?

No, it would go unnoticed.

That goes without saying.

Truth *means* "truth said."

That's true. You said it!

THE FAILURE OF PRODUCTIVE COMMERCE BE-TWEEN ADVERTISING AND TRUTH; THEIR ESSEN-TIAL VOID OF COMMUNICATION, AS BEING TOTALLY UNALIKE

Advertising makes a thing seem more than it is.

That's what the advertisers *try* to do.

And they've learned how successful to be.

The consumers are easily duped.

They *want* to be. Their already-set-up demand is temptingly *confirmed* by the wizardry of advertising; which readily declares, "Look what's available!" to inform an inclined market how to fulfill its purchasing tendencies.

Those are helpful suggestions. But the distortions of truth employed! The information falsified! Those misleading leads! Those emotionalized exaggerations! Those carefully stressed inaccuracies, those beguiling inducements, those deceptive flairs! These are publicity-facts, publicity-metaphors! All colored.

The "emphases" are intentional. The public is deliberately "guided," given "beneficial" hints. Purchasing is "assisted;" language misused. But what can we do? Advertising is here to stay.

I know what we can do!

What?

We can bend over backwards, and make *less* of the advertised good or service, in proportion as the ad makes *more* of it. If *they* stretch the truth *one* way, *we* stretch it the opposite—in the precise degree! That way, we rectify the imbalance.

It would strain our minds. We'd always have to be reading magazines and newspapers, listening to the radio, watching television, observing signs everywhere—billboards, posters, window displays. Even watching airplane smoke-ads above! It wouldn't do. For we'd be doing nothing else. Our life would be unnaturally obsessed, and laden with distress. *I* know of an *easier* way.

What?

To correct the subtle blatancy of advertising, what we should do is this, simply: never buy or use anything whatever advertised. Even such utilities as electricity and water. Any food whatever. All clothing. Shoes, soap, reading matter, residential dwellings, any service or convenience or article of necessity in any way advertised. That'll rid advertising of us. Our consuming days will be over. And the days themselves, too.

Will we be dead?

Yes. Survived by advertising. As the greater survives the smaller, the dragon outlives the snail. Our consuming matter will be subsumed by the void's consumption. Our needs and appetites will be themselves devoured, and our demands yielded up. As perishable products and marked-down items, we'll find ourselves swallowed up in huge advertising's massive depository maw, that wants more and more, seizing ceaselessly with mechanical veracity in the wasteful obsolescing of economy's growing turnovers with enlarged profit churned out at the other end.

What a crude end! And refined advertising will carry on?

The strategy is deliberate, and backed by the marked instruments of objective science itself, for company gain, agency prestige, and beneficial business cooperation that boosts sales and promotes more production. It's bigger than both of us, however we protest.

How unhappy for us! We're outweighed!

What can we do? Be martyrs of futility, and as a final act, equate protest with death, in solutions of suicidal purity against the world's conscience? Would that produce the slightest metaphysical effect, toward changing the order?

No; then let's live and remain in the irritation and imperfection of our commercial system. Let's live, amid posters. If there's no Truth about, we'll support it in *imagination*. There'll always be a Truth. If advertising drives it off the world, we'll find it elsewhere. We'll be devoted to follow it, in exile. We'll administer to its refugee alienation from its old factual home, where the Dictator now rules. And we'll plot an overthrow, however idealistic. Truth will go underground, and its supporters will sneak it subsistence. Some day, its lost honor will find revenge. The turning wrath will re-install disinterested Truth, to benefit no one in gain's exploitation or as applied to pursuits of practical personal advantage, social advancement, and those vain, rationalized irresponsibilities of business enlightenment philanthropic to worldly ends. The Truth will have a spiritual renaissance; advertising will be secured by secular limbo, in a temporal banishment. As, now, *Truth* seems banished; and as its travelling fellows, we're forced to follow it into hiding where business can't root it out and stamp it with a trademark, brand it to label, and exhibit it in captivity like a prisoner of the thronging Romans, as packages and cartons roll by for the democratic citizens to behold and partake, thinking themselves lucky. Truth is as neutral as water. And just as unadvertisable.

But water *is* advertised. In various forms, basic and secondary. And man is advertised. God, as well. And so are ideals. All higher things, have been advertised.

Oh. Do we condone advertising, then?

No. Let's support the things in *our* way, before advertising distorts them.

That means a fresh evaluation of everything for ourselves, independent of popular "usage." A tough job, this independent re-appraising. Not a task I'd call enviable.

Let's take it on. Truth would reward us. You'll see.

Truth? It's powerless, now! So how would it be *able* to reward us?

By inflicting delight. And beauty. It's all to the good.

Can Truth do all that, even when out of power?

Yes. Humanity, when raised high, responds to it with special happiness. So let's cultivate our humanity, to get the most out of truth: which can afford a great deal for the ultimate state of our well-being.

Fine. Shall we then prepare an advertisement for Truth, inserting it in some appropriate medium that would project its convincing message to the broadest possible circulation in a prime vehicle for mass audience, conveying a hard-sell gospel against mince minds?

No. It's self-proclaiming. That's how it holds so much merit, in its intrinsic qualities. The essence comes through, all by itself. Not needing a nudge by props and pimps. It's self-illuminating. Self-sustaining. Self-sufficient. Its own internal grace gets crystal radiation.

In transparence? Not needing to be glossed over, lacquered, varnished, pepped up, dolled out, adorned, spoken for, made scintillating, injected with gleaming impressiveness, decked out becomingly, set to music, tuned up, furnished with artificial appeal, endorsed by fashion, enriched by publicity, garnished, extolled, lauded, boosted, boasted, beset with decorations, rewarded in strains of embellishment, brought out in style, enticingly coated, sponsored into polished sheen, shiningly shown forth in amplified magnitudes of flattering metaphor and parabola'ed to parable and fabled fabulous and done smart and slicked up and translated to charm, shaped pretty, beamingly broadcast, well presented, proudly proclaimed, unhesitatingly acclaimed, dearly recommended, given ample testimony, doctored up, scientifically backed, tested impartially, proven beyond doubt, unadulterated with praise, in guaranteed formula, and popularized in laboratory specialization under technical expertise, to bring out its utmost extravagance in the most excelling terms, scaled upward from a superlative basis, ritualized by adaptation into the occult magic of a simple, clear, sensible universal, a wonder and marvel for civilization's optimistic progress, which a child can operate, it's so natural by law as a miracle-working cosmetic.

The cosmic is anti-cosmetic. Advertising washes out. Truth remains, though we rub hard. We can't get rid of it.

Do we *want* to get rid of it?

At times it's unbearable. Unlike advertising, which is made palatable, and appetizing, with gracious and soft appeal that earns an easy victory. The truth is tough. And never victorious, not needing to sell itself. It only *is*.

Without glory?

Yes, but not inglorious. Beyond the shallowness of glorification.

Advertising is easier to take. It sparkles so nicely, sprinkling gilt-dust and benediction on the items luckily blessed as advertised, endowed to such fortunate representation, purring out the cosy world.

Truth is an unlazy proposition. We must overcome *ourselves*, to approach a position to appreciate it. Let's make circumstances compatible to it. Let's relate conditions to its stern absolute, and brace ourselves to its rigorous vigors, as live substance, not dead art.

By dead art, you imply advertising?

Or the vacuum's artifice. The void's craft. Ugly device. A practical contraption. Never disinterested, ever below the gratuitous, with a lurking purpose. The truth doesn't help our affairs. It has no use. It's inactive. It's a luxury.

I thought it was *spare*, not luxurious.

We can't put it to use. That places it above. We would be noble, to pursue it, then.

It defies personal advantage?

By not giving us a functionable service. There it is. It's by itself.

Are you its promoter?

How can I *deal* in it? It's not to be owned. Not even transferred. It has momentary value. It strokes the mind, and disarms us of utilizing it. We think it. That's all.

Can't it be consumed, fulfilled, tapped, realized, productive? Is it not even creative?

It only *is*, poor thing. And when exploitation is intended, it skips past. It has an air-like freedom. It's strikingly intangible. You can't touch it.

Isn't there *concrete* truth?

I'm referring to unempirical truth. Good only at the mind's worth. It goes bad on act's coarseness, at the sour world's application, in the gross livery of product. It serves no necessity, answers no need, fosters no want, advances no cause. Truth is non-personal. It lacks advertising's appeal.

Truth is a very unsexual thing. Not even the tiniest magnetism. No. So deprived. A collection ought to fund-raise it from the poverty level. Advertising is vast. And rich. It commands such resources, of notorious wealth, unlimited enterprise, resorting to whole industries of incentive, whole careers of will, intense vanities immensely reposed in exhaustively trained ambition. It disposes empires, with reserves to spare. Advertising is infinite. And by comparison, what is truth? A pauper with no worldly belonging. A knave of privilege, a serf of unsuperiority. It can offer us nothing by any world's standard. But, being no beggar, it's begged for, and in vain, by the whole world.

A PICKPOCKET SELF-EXPOSED

The height of futility is a thief pickpocket who wears transparent clothes so that his booty-lined pockets are transparently see-through. He must be suffering from a "confession complex." Such self-defeatism would almost be inspired, were it not so transparently obvious. He obviously has misgivings about his profession. It's like turning his pockets out, to turn himself in. He stains his own name, by treading upon his own trade. Perhaps he was cut out for a different line of aptitude. He could be a window display dresser, by choice. Certainly, as a pickpocket, he demonstrates a glaring honesty unbecoming to a thief's honor. Success should be undertaken along with any given path of endeavor. Otherwise, he turns a thief upon himself. He makes it criminally easy, for the police.

PROTECTING PRIVATE DOUBT AGAINST SOCIAL AS-SURANCE

I'd rather not speculate in dubious explanations as a social par-lor game in which indeterminacy and doubt are considered in-tolerable acts of defiant anti-sociability.

So when asked "why" I'm sad, I'll reply "I don't know." The empty, ritualistic greeting "How are you," or the empty, ritual-istic settling-in-for-a-long-chat "How have you been?" are also to be rejected with "I don't know." This reply protects the per-sonal incompleteness from the socially requisite "Here it is; of course I know it all."

Better remain privately mute and dumb than to glibly but falsely "play the game."

(Title of abstract dialogue, of unusual length in proportion to the dialogue it entitles:)

THINGS SO NAMED ARE NAMED THINGS, NO LONGER THE THINGS THEY WERE. WORDS AFFECT THE MIND. EACH MIND IS CENTRAL, TO EVERYTHING THOUGHT ANYWHERE AT ANY TIME PAST OR TO BE, DUE TO THE GREAT HOOK-UP. WE'RE ONE SPECIES; WITH EACH CELL "UNIQUE." NAMES BIND TIME AND SPACE IN MADE MAGIC. WORDS HAVE ENTRY TO ANY-THING INFINITE OR ETERNAL—AND EXIT INTO THE SAME. A WHOLE UNIVERSAL SOUL OF MAN HAS LO-CAL POSTS IN EACH MIND. THE MIND HAS ORGA-NIZED OURSELVES TO EVERY SOCIAL AGE AND CON-DITION, SINCE IT'S CENTRAL TO EVERY OUTPOST AND IS COMMUNALLY SHARED, LIKE THE COM-MUNAL WELL OR MARKET PLACE IN PRIMITIVE UNITS. WE'RE LINKED UP. YET WHY DO WE FEEL LONELY? LET'S GIVE LONELINESS A NEW WORD—IT MAY CHANGE, FOR BETTER OR WORSE. MEAT RE-MAINS MEAT. THINGS *ARE* NAMES: AND CHANGE, ACCORDINGLY.

Growing meat is a fruitless task.

Why?

Because meat isn't fruit.

At least, is meat meat?

It sure is. Otherwise it wouldn't be *named* meat.

What *would* it be named?

If meat were not meat?

Yeah?

It would be named something else: it would be given the name of what it *is*—not what it isn't.

But what it is is more limited than what it's *not*.

That's why it should be given a specific name to pinpoint and "fix" the limited thing it is, defining it off discriminately against all the numerously unlimited things that it falls into the category of *not being*.

So names fend off the looseness of chaos?

Yes, or hopefully do so.

What if a thing has been named something for years, or even centuries, and then suddenly that thing displays radical new qualities and loses the attributes it's been *traditionally* known for? What happens to the name: does the name undergo new corresponding connotations to keep itself in accuracy as a name?

Yes. So if a respectable man is suddenly exposed as a criminal of bribery, graft, and corruption, he's said to have lost his "good name."

And does the Moon connote something different now that men have recently landed and walked on it?

Decidedly. It's not quite the same old "Moon."

Yet if we read of the Moon in a work of literature predating the Moon landing, we're capable of reading in the old archaic meaning, necessary for the appreciation of the passage.

Yes, precisely. We honor history and tradition, venerate retrospect, and are capable of identifying with ideas and realities current to ancient periods but not to our own. We're flexibly sympathetic, and are capable of impersonal references. Our comprehension can leap out of our own time, if need be: allowing some literature to be timeless, and always timely.

That's fine, I'm glad. We have such sweep, such scope. We can look behind and before, and not be limited to now. I'm proud, of such accomplishments.

And it keeps us in touch with all the dead and all the not-yet-born. The mind is collective, not just collectively contemporaneous with our contemporaries, but collective to the past, and to the unknown to be. The mind is our human cohesive agent that binds us to all fellow men however far away in place or period. The mind is our civilizing unity, our cultural gatherer into a center. For each mind is a center to what's common property to all. The most private ideas become social commonwealth. Each mind is a local post receptive to all the "generals" that flow and reflow and reach all levels. Each mind is the specific outpost for the All, and everything passes into each mind, through it, and into All. The center is located in each being. We're hooked up by network, it's a world community, binding together the globe and the whole pile of centuries in which each individual human "cell" feels the shared glory of the unique.

Your description I found idealistic, too glowing with hope, unnaturally lit up. I have gloomier ways of appraisal, that seem closer to "the way things are." Your transports postulated the exalted "should"—and so seem, to use a modern term, unrealistic.

You're right too, in your own way: a darker truth. But mine lives too, my way: for my mind lives. We're all right; "wrong" is irrelevant. When we think a thing to be, it becomes that. Words ensure we're right. We use names, and so "create" "realities." Words are mental magic; (the mind's magic illumines words). Meat is meat. It's all there, in the name.

PICASSO'S LATE FIXATION-DEVELOPMENT

Picasso got to the point where he can't see anything flat anymore, so everything is sculptured in the round that he can lay his brush on, or his feet, head, fingers, or whatever. He's sterilized to a round point.

WHAT'S HE THINKING OF NOW? QUOTE HIS IDEAS INTO WORDS, AS THESE STRUGGLE TO FLY.

He conceives of fiction as poetically bridging across to philosophy, where poetic ideals "ultimate." "Man tries to resolve his disorderly feelings by arranging ideas into temporary bodies of truth. He tries to go from a confusion of emotional memories to the momentary sublime relief of some philosophical 'concrete'. From mute mental pain to an articulated artifice where some brief high pleasure is tastable. Then all collapses, and he's lost again. That's unbearable, so he picks up his pieces and tries for a new thought edifice. He won't give up, but shoves consciousness ahead again."

WAILINGS OF A SKEPTIC. (MY INCREDULITY IS UNLEASHED—AND GOES SNARLING, TO BITE ITS IMAGINARY TARGETS)

Why is the truth always trying to form itself as a paradox? This indicates a showing-off tendency: as though the truth had too much self-doubt (or inferiority complex) to afford to let itself be "seen" without the embellishment of some startling shape that calls attention to "the way it's put"—form, in fact, over content.

Does the truth suspect that ungarnished content is insufficient to carry much weight with the reader or listener it's trying to impress?

Why must the truth garb itself in impressiveness?: as though it were ashamed of itself naked, unadorned, plain?

Is it because the truth is competing with other truths for the reader's or listener's limited and often bored attention? Like, in a subway car, a horizontal row of forty consecutive, disconnected, and mutually competing advertisement panels, each trying to be brilliant with color, shock, surprisingness, audacity, sensationalism, pornography, self-proclaiming, like a mating call trying to be unique and successful in a whole chorus of mating calls by the massed gender of that species—for the single response of a lone representative of the opposite gender. God, is the market so stacked!?

Or like girls' dressing themselves in a self-advertising fashion in competition with other girls in the same ballroom.

Oh, Truth, how you demean yourself when you force me to compare you with those demeaning things! Have you no pride, no integrity, no "strength of humility," to permit yourself modesty rather than garishness of taste? Are you essentially a vulgarian, Truth?—the way you try to pop through the lavish, dyed color and starched glitter of your stuffed shirt that's too big for your breeches? What are you trying to hide?—the Truth of yourself, Truth?

All puffed out, like an empty toad? All inflated, like a tartish show-off with disproportionate and imported breasts to attract the tourist sailor trade?

Shame on you, Truth! If not too late, revert to your maiden modesties, with which you were originally and eternally invested.

Resist the temptation to outdo the modesty of your own nature, Truth. You haven't gone into the publicity or public-relations fields as your own agent and your own client trying to "tag" yourself with a popular image that can "catch on," like a cheap tune to tinkle the unrefined ear? Is the whole thing an advertising game for you, in which the "public appearance" of a thing is more the point than the essence and intrinsic qualities of that thing?

Truth, you've Sold Out! You're a fink!

You've betrayed your birthright, Truth! And what have you gained, for that infamous self-betrayal? The cheapening of yourself, that's all.

No, that's *not* all. You've confused issues, muddled identity, perverted values, falsified essences. You've weaved the spell of a veil of blurs to eradicate what things are—for the sake of appearances. Only appearances count, with you. They deceive, they spread illusions, they're self-deceptive, they undermine the people's confidence in "things as they are."

"The truth will out." Yes, it's already *gone* out—of fashion.

Never to return? Oh, I'm nostalgic for you, Truth. I'll revisit you, in some past age—when your form was less deceptive.

I want you to be you—it's all for your own sake that I'm mourning so—mourning your demise in this age, Truth, when you've outdone yourself, or done yourself in, through a lack of shining faith, a failure of belief.

Goodby, Truth; till we meet again: in shapes more befitting ourselves, you and your believer.

I trust you'll emerge, eventually, "as yourself," as it were: recognizable. Till then, I don't acknowledge you, in your ersatz molds. You've lost a believer. I hereby officially suspend credulity—till you reappear in a way that gains my confidence.

My loss is great—for, having lost confidence in you, Truth, what about my own poor self? I'm predicated, as a self, on faith in truth. That faith shaken (or suspended, or broken, or waived for the time), then I'm not me, anymore. *For what am I, unless I relate, Truth, to you?*

Time & Place

TIME AND ETERNITY

(For some inscrutable reason the organisers of the Southbank Poetry International Festival in London, summer of '73, invited Marvin Cohen onto the platform.)

By the way, the poet I'm following is Basil Bunting, and the poet who's following is Hugh MacDiarmid. So what am *I* doing here? Anyway, what's the common denominator between me and them? I'll tell you. It's Queen Elizabeth Hall, which has now finally done its job in expressing democracy.

This is supposed to be a poetry reading, but I don't even know if I'm a poet. I don't know *what* I am. But I must be *something*, otherwise how could I be here tonight in front of you? So let's leave it at that, with the obscure solidity of my tall form being looked at by you, and my mid-Atlantic monotones being heard by you, which completes the audience-performer relationship on a formal one-to-many basis.

I suppose I'm supposed to read from something I wrote, but everything I wrote bores me, because I wrote it in the past, and now it's now. What I wrote in the *past* doesn't fit in with the present situation. It seems dead and unvital compared to the living throbbing moment of all of us here assembled in Queen Elizabeth Hall in, as it were, the Los Angeles part of Europe. Most of us are the audience, a few of us are the performers. So yesterday I wrote an essay about this occasion to make what I say appropriate to this very situation that unites us all. And now, without further ado or fuss of fanfare, let me begin. If I don't soon begin, it'll be too late, because Charles Osborne, the Arts Council organiser of this event, has only allotted me fifteen minutes, so I better hurry. So you keep along with me, and you hurry too.

(When I say hurry, I don't mean you should hurry out of this auditorium to leave me speaking here alone; that would be rude. I mean to hurry up while you're still sitting down. To keep your seats and still hurry means only one thing: that the hurrying you're doing is a *mental* hurry. And let me *direct* your mental hurry. But I better hurry.)

Consciousness is why we're all here tonight. When you hear these poets read, a more or less common bond of consciousness unites all us listeners with the poet who reads, thanks to the good old link of unity called language.

A primary thing about consciousness is its going along in time. (And words often keep it company, or follow ideas as points of crystallization.) So when one of these poets starts reading, we all start listening to him at the same rate of his reading to us. (Not quite, since a word he's reading occurs slightly *before* that word is being heard by us, due to the slowness it takes sound to travel. But we should accept that imperfection gracefully and not complain, simply because complaint couldn't not alter such an iron-bound reality as the time gap between a word spoken and the same word being heard. So be a conservative and don't protest.)

Anyway, one of these poets starts reading and we're hearing the beginning of what he's saying. He's giving us ideas through words, a flow of ideas through a *flow* of words, a *progression* of ideas through a *progression* of words. The *continuity*, the *sequence*, the *building up*, occur to all of us in common with him, since the *order* of the words, the *order* of the ideas, is the same order for all of us who listen, in common with him, since the *order* of the words, the *order* of the ideas, is the same order for all of us who listen, in common with each other who listen, and in common with the poet who *delivers* that order. As with a symphony being played or an opera performed, the poem being read is made possible, not through the auspices of the Arts Council of Great Britain, but through the auspices of *Time*. Therefore, on behalf of all of us gathered here tonight, I wish to extend a formal thank-you to Time and its generous offices. Thank you, Time. Keep it up. In fact, keep *us* up, by not running us out of our lives too soon.

Time keeps everything from happening all at once. It lets us put the left foot forward and *then* the right foot, enabling us to walk due to a time gap between one foot forward and *then* the next. Otherwise, it would be like our ankles were tied together in a potato sack and we'd have to jump like a frog all the time, which is a natural way for the frog but awkward for us.

So anyway, one of these poets, let's say, is in the middle of reading one of his long poems. While we're listening to the words he's reading from the middle of his poem, we ourselves are "reading in" (as it were) to his reading of the middle,—all that we remember in the series and order of ideas from the *beginning* of that same poem. Therefore, we're *co-operating* with the poet who's reading, by extending him the *courtesy* of remembering what he's read of the poem *so far*. He ought to be grateful and pay *us*. Instead, we had to pay him, because the tickets were so expensive to let us into Queen Elizabeth Hall in the Waterloo section of the British Empire. But it's too late to object, because we *already* paid for our tickets, so we may as well try to tolerate this deliberately arranged and organized evening of institutional poetry institutionally read, even though that same poetry *originated* not institutionally but privately in the private individual inspiration of each poet's solitary head.

Finally, I'm about to finish up. Thanks for bearing with me so far. If we got as far as this, let's plug on, and round it out with a suitable ending. I'm very *dependent* on your continuing to listen—more dependent than *you* are on my continuing to read. So you see, you have the upper hand.

(Pardon me for addressing you collectively as an audience. I know each one of you is individual, but I don't have time to grant a private audience with each one of you in turn and keep repeating my speech over and over personally to you one at a time. That would long exceed my time limit here at Queen Elizabeth Hall, in a politically weak country that used to be so politically strong. Therefore, regrettably, I resort to a manufacturing device. But instead of manufacturing a lot of identical goods via the same economical process as in mass production assembly line, which is a spatial thing involving spatial commodities, I speak *simultaneously* for all of you *collectively at once*, thus insulting you by reducing each one of your individualities to a *herd* figure. (Actually, *I'm* the herd figure, for you hear me, therefore I'm *heard*. I'm glad I filled you in on the *scene*.))

Time is my theme. I hope time keeps pace with me, in its timely fashion. I'm not so self-reliant or self-sufficient as to pretend to give this speech unassisted by time. I hope you forgive me for this weakness of relying on time. But where would this speech be without time? I mean *when* would this speech be without time?, not *where*. *When* is time's property, not where. That's why when someone fills my glass from a bottle of alcohol, they always say "Say when!" They don't say "Say where"—they can see my glassware. If while they're pouring I cleverly delay saying "When," then—"my cup brimmeth over," which is an antiquated expression of time-worn ecstasy.

Time is one thing after another. How can I say that *backwards*? Easy: Time is one thing before another.

But "thing" is arbitrary, the lumping together into *substantive* shape and form (notice the *spatial* terminology) of interpenetrating events that merge by *transitive* degrees in the flow of time's succession.

By the way, the previous paragraph contained no humor. Therefore, you did right not to laugh: you were right on cue. I hope you'll be *equally* expert in finding the right time to laugh. But I'll leave it up to you. No speaker should *bully* his audience, which so vastly outnumbers him, here, in Queen Elizabeth Hall, which is part of an island that's played a substantial role so far in the history of Western Civilization: and I hope it never ends, especially not tonight.

However, my *speech* is coming to an end. It's defied all the preconceived ideas of expectation and anticipation of what it was going to be. Soon, as soon as I stop, all it will be will be only a memory. But the memory of it will vary according to each person who remembers it, just like an article of furniture is different when you put it into one room compared to the way it is when put into another room—especially if the other room is in a different house—like *your* house, for example.

Also, what anyone of you remembers about this speech will alter as time goes on. When I *stop* speaking, there will be an immediate afterglow that trails behind it like a wake behind a ship, swelling out behind it, dissolving into time. Then *another* reader will read, and you'll pay attention to *him*. All intervening events and experiences in your own lives between my speech and the *next* time you remember my speech, will that much alter the memory of my speech. And my speech meanwhile will have its little lump intermingled with all you ever underwent since birth—or even maybe before, who knows? Next week, in a wholly new context, you'll have your latest now. *In* that now, my speech will have gone through transformations of layers of memory, each new remembrance containing the sum of all previous remembrances *plus itself*. So you see, time distorts.

Time distorts past events, but does not distort thought. Thought, as it's being thought in the now, is its *own* distortion— therefore it's direct.

Thought is absent matter. Thought is a person or event that's *not there*—thought *substitutes* for the *presence* of the person or event you're thinking of, in the form of memory, regret, remorse, grief, hope, expectation, longing, desire, fear, anxiety, and the inventiveness of the imagination. The imagination is only there when we're not perceiving an event or object. But it surrounds all perceptions. Most of life is in waiting impatiently, tided over by daydreams of fear or desire, and the million phases and stages of hope, for something that's not yet, that's yet to be, and that, when it *does* occur, will differ absolutely from all the preceding thoughts, images, and feelings *about* it, toward it, and before it. We fear, desire, and expect, according to what we *remember. Most* of life is *remembering* things, desiring to repeat them or avoid them, and reckoning, on the basis of remembering, on what we hope, expect, and dread.

It's about *time*, my speech has been. And it's *about time*, that it should end.

Therefore, as we're all in Queen Elizabeth Hall, where politics would never wish to stray, and where *men* tread, not *angels*, I must set this as our site. We're all dying, thanks to time. But time, in its mercy, *delays* our dying, retards our decay, to spin things out, to richly unfurl or feebly unfold our feelings and events, so that we have time for suffering, misery, joy, boredom, hope, desire, memory, anxiety, the majority banality and the minority sublimity.

Now, just a word about the nature of the "now."

Each new now reconstructs, according to its own mood and use, according to our own newest needs and newest attitudes, all that went before, including previous remembered events. Every new now is a new retrospect of what was, and a new set of future possibilities. We only have one now at a time. But time is a renewed succession of now after now after now. Each now is a doubt. That's why we ask, *"Now* what?" Each now is uncertain and undetermined. Each now is incomplete. That's why we need later nows to try to complete this now. (For example, that's why my speech is still going on and hasn't stopped.) But those later nows are *still* incomplete and indeterminate. This is why eternity is an ideal, to give us a resting place from the incessant successive dissatisfactions of all our nows. We construct eternity and the absolute as ideal havens from all the uncertainties of flux. We want to be free from the perils and hazards of chance, Mystery, Unknown. We want to fix and arrest flow into what is sure and known. (Known already, the *prior* known.) We look for what endures, to feel more secure. We're looking for a halt. Time is too much for us. We need courage and fortitude to combat *all* of time. For relief, we dream of *Eternity's* sublime solace.

Now I'm going to deflate a popular idol: Eternity. I'm going to extol time at Eternity's expense. I hope this doesn't upset any traditional religious or philosophical notion, and thereby create discomfort. However, I'm here to create discomfort. It's in the essence of anything new that it *disturbs*. The new is contrary to the remembered, to the familiar. So if I create discomfort, forgive me. I'm only human, like you. *I* like satisfaction better than dissatisfaction, too. But when the new takes over, previous complacencies of the predictable, to feel secure within a system or structure that may always be relied on. The indeterminate is too risky an enemy. That's why new ideas are enemies of middle class security. They threaten to upset structures in which emotional comfort has been invested, to perpetuate emotional comfort at the expense of the *unsettling*.

I hate whatever's trendy. However, here comes my blast, as well, against the *opposite* of trendiness: against that time-honored spiritual monument, Eternity.

I dedicate this speech to time. I wish time well. I hope it gets what it wants. But what *does* time want? Does time aspire to eternity? *No!* Eternity aspires to *time*. But eternity is too thick and hide-bound, like an obsolete old vehicle of war too cumbersome to be maneuvered; too thick and hide-bound is eternity, to be able to attain its desired condition of time. Time is deft, quick, supple, like guerrilla warfare, time is adaptable: eternity is unwieldy, slow, crude, and gross. Time is eternity's superior. Eternity will never reverse that status and usurp time. Therefore Eternity pouts like Iago and puts on airs—puts on airs of being *absolute*. But it's only being pretentious. Only time is real—because only time is *modest* enough to be real. Eternity's immodest, presumptuous bombast makes it ridiculously unreal. That's why this speech will stop eternally, which only went on in time.

Not only did this speech go on in time—it went on, as well, in Queen Elizabeth Hall. But where is Queen Elizabeth Hall? It's in time, just like us.

A FABLE WITH A STILL MORAL

Who came first—time or the clock? "I," said time; "I," said the clock; and they flew round in lively debate.

Man was called in to decide, and chose to honor both; so he stepped out of life; and the combatants, to mourn him, concluded fast, and stopped. Thus Peace won out and was well rid of all three.

THE POET, THE CRITIC—INCOMPATIBLE

The poet creates *out of* the past; the critic criticizes him *from* the past, *against* the past—conservatively (unfairly, too; uncomprehendingly, often arrogantly, often with hostility).

The poet leaps on, The critic points to the past and yells that it's violated. Don't listen, poet. Listen *in*ward, not to *him*.

HEARING A LECTURE IN PASSAGE THROUGH FROM THE EARLY PAST TO THE LATE PAST TOWARD THE NEXT LATEST OF ALL THOSE ACCUMULATED NOWS IN EACH OF TWO DRIVING LIVES OWNED PRIVATELY APART BY MY FRIEND AND ME, GIVEN A WORLD APIECE FOR TIME TO CHASE US THROUGH.

Just where were we living? When not including ourselves, it was in the world. Couldn't we know it? Yes, but how? A lecture. Then, watch our understanding grow!

"Hurry up," swiftly alerted my friend: "we have tickets to a modern lecture about the world today. There's seating room only, so we stand in the back row on the middle aisle right close to the speaker's platform, where a brave lecture, as yet unannounced, will give a social commentary all about the way the world is, and how, thereby, life is universally affected. Man will be seen in context, and prophecy will be attempted, based on the fallen mistakes of our slovenly past deeds, as well as moral pronouncements, and verdicts fatal to mankind's industry. Hear the speaker for tonight place the troubled weight of judgment on these the shallow shoulders of our falling-apart day and age, a lucid demonstration of what we've come to, offering the hopeful, if not benign, conclusion that there is no way out, and the way in is already locked up, keeping us in a suspended state of entrapment, while bravely, to pass the time away, we deteriorate."

"But is the lecture free?" I first asked. "Yes, but it costs plenty," warned my careful friend, knowing what the tickets were reserving for us. So by hurrying, and panting our breath along, we arrived too soon, and so were totally late, if not irrevocably tardy, providing we were there at all, sooner or later, being timely placed at the right where, and not placed out of time in the broad world of anywhere. Anyway, so there we were. The speaker himself lives outside description, but the delivered words spoken that night are preserved here in the original semblance of their sequence, and the order intended is placed under the scrutiny of duplication, as far as my friend and I deliberately heard or inconclusively understood:

"The world! It's something, isn't it? There's only one way to go. Out. Goodbye, ladies and gentlemen. And I may add, good night."

(With that, the villain smiled. He knew he had scored. The audience attended their collective guilt. For an encore, before evaporating, their bewilderer added, from depths previously unseen and levels inlaid with miraculous veils of invisibility borrowed from the occult astral sphere of superstition, "Don't forget your breath. It's your one invaluable substance. Lose it, and our world is careless, packed into a fading past. Look ahead, in the event you stop. Aren't the views beautiful? Life is poetry, inside. And on the opening out, how empty we are, in the breathless mirror of the world! Unkind, isn't it? Well, bother your sins, and go." At that, the doors opened. Some sigh was heaved, and God was thought of, in modern terms of futility. Nothing more?)

No, nothing. We left the lecture hall, full of what had just passed. Then the leaving passed, too. And where are we?

IN TIME—BUT HOPING *OUT.* THE ENSLAVED SOUL'S NOSTALGIA FOR ITS PRE-TIME CONDITION. BUT TIME BINDS IT TO ITS WILL. IT SURROUNDS THE SLAVE WITH ITS DENSE CLOUD, AND HE CAN'T SEE THROUGH, ANGUISH, STRUGGLE, AGONY— THEN SUBMISSION. BUT THE DEFIANT VISION PERSISTS—TO UN-TIME ITSELF, AND COME OUT, CLEAN THROUGH. IN THAT HOPE, THE SLAVE EN-DURES HIS LOT, AND LOSES HIS ONLY LIFE TO AN EARTH OF TIME.

I joined time by being conceived. Before that, my existence could not have been understood by *people*, for people are time-animals whose ideas are by time's terms and whose whole lives in each detail are time-tied and time-determined.

Before I too became a time-monster like every other hu-man person, I was a non-time entity.

(The fact that I'm a person makes me use the biased human negative, "non-time entity," for only in time's terms can I even begin to conceive or, however dimly, recall, anything of a non-time nature—a concept remote to the human mind for whom time is like water to a fish. A fish *lives* in water, by water, from water—its heaven or hell destination is watery too, as well as its lifelong fate. All non-wet terms sound a bit fishy to it. Ob-viously, it "knows" what its element is. How foreign must any successfully communicated essence of fire, air, or earth seem, to the fish that's truly true to its own nature! Circumscribed in its mental range, restricted within its own interest-code, the fish obeys its limitations, which define the natural disciplined circles, the free rules and zones, where it may swim and be.)

Pardon me for the underwater digression, which I've taken responsibility for by marking it off in parentheses. Now, to re-sume my theme, which is, to talk to time-beings in time's terms of a non-time condition. That's so difficult to do, I'm hardly to blame for escaping by way of digression from so impossible an attempt. I'm tempted to digress again, so averse am I to deal with a non-time topic in even negatively timely terms. I'm neither God nor miracle man: therefore I shrink with modesty from a task so titanic. Like a fish, *I'm* bound by my limits, too.

I see time, sniff it, hear it, touch it, feel it—I'm floating in its skin. But I've a past before it: I was nude of it, once.

That was before conception by my sexually bound mother and father which ignited my being into this sphere of time. This sphere of time is all I am, all I know. Once, though, it wasn't so. Let me trace that dim vague "source." Let me regress, ere time was.

What was I, in the non-time sphere? Time kills my "memory" of it, for time is king of all memory. And time defends its interests. It would be against time's interest to permit so "disloyal-and-unpatriotic-to-time's-kingdom" an act of heresy as my "recollection" (as it were) of some pagan pre-time reign.

I'm subjected to Time's spell by thrall to its unfathomableness. It keeps me in line, by suspending me in mystery, to weave its enchantment. I'm governable by my ignorance. The system has watchguards, including the subject's own conscience from within, to catch him overturning Time's law in insurrection or rebellion. The punishment is severe: offenders are shoved off Time's plank, under tight blindfold and the booming kettledrums and the cannon roar and the fife's trembling little lament, down down into a sea of drowning as death rips off the body and the soul is stripped of memory to be "purged" clean and white prior to its next stage of metamorphosis devoid of a clue as to what its previous stage had been, in what garb but where.

"Where" is time.

"Where" *usually* pertains to place. Time, however, has conquered place, and now uses the imperial "where" in its pomp and office of state.

So Time is where we are. "How" and "why" are involved in the "where." "Where" has usurped, assimilated, all of "when"'s connotation.

"Where" is omnipresent. Its omnipotence is by its omnipresence, Its omniscience is too. How ominous it is!

"Where" is everywhere. "Locality" is too slight for it. Just like the mighty Express subway train in the majestic New York subway system shows lordly disdain of deigning to stop at a slovenly little *local* station stop, so too, in likewise, Time is too big, too everywhere-at-the-same-time, to stoop to mere "locality."

"On location," a film is shot. *Time* films itself *off* location. It knows only of astronomical magnitudes. Why should it go about on a lesser scale of grandeur? Time is the humbler of man. Man can't imitate Time, only envy it, resent it, stand in awe, and submit.

But I intend to *defy* Time.

I was born Time's slave, on earth "here"; but by birthright of legacies in prior forms of before-Time being and pre-earth migration, I'm proudly free, my spirit untied to Time's tyranny. I wish to return to that former magnificence. But my human-earth habit prevents my memory from diving off the backward of my original earth conception at the mating of my two parents. I can't recapture the non-Time before that—retrospect ends at that vital juncture, that key transition mark. Oh, I feel so deprived! I *long* for what went before, as an out-of-Time entity. My mind is fogged down to Time, and can't recall.

I struggle but in vain to reclaim my spiritual legacy as a being unbesotted by Time's grime, impervious to its cult of pollution. I enlist magic, but I fail to see before Time was. It's all a blank to me, I draw a blank though I invoke with plea. My Muse-addressed invocation to bless me with divine intervention and see me through my by-no-means-mean task, went unanswered; So I'm all alone, in Time—in my enemy's land. I can't see back. Like a fish in sea, I'm too immersed in my element; I swim and grow organs in it, and it binds me all about. I can't see *through* Time, to translate its opacity in transcendent transparency. So I'm thickly-woven in, hemmed and sealed off. I wished for an off-sight; and am consoled with only a base *in*sight. I'm Time's, it's not mine. It outlasts me, and is larger. I Joined it, for a while. I'm spending a term here—on *its* terms. I'm sentenced for a spell. I was conceived, to die. My past is lost. My future will be, but I won't be in it—not anyway as I am. It'll be a *new being's* future; not mine. I'm only here, and now. *So* finite. So *only* me.

I accept my limits now. I submit, let Time will. I'm me for now and here. To travel off, and wander—and retreat historically to my pre-personal "person". That's all my yearning, but never done.

EARLY LESSONS IN KNOWING YOUR PLACE AND BE-ING HUMBLE IN IT

There are so many more things that you are not, than there are the things that you are. Think of all that you are not. They include negative and positive possibilities. In other words, everything—except you.

Whatever is left, is you. Left over, from what? From the all that is not you.

And the tiny you that *is*: is in a tiny *time*, too. Of all the time spanning before you, spanning after you—the tiny trail of time *not* included, is *your* time.

The time you have, and the you that you are: that's all. That's all for *you*.

You are as tiny as what you have. *Outside* of that—don't you wish you were *there*?

THREE OUTBURSTS OF TIME

1. AUTOBIOGRAPHY STRIPPED OF FACTS

I used to have intense philosophical moments. They became physical, which enriched the philosophy. Then they became too physical, and the philosophy stopped. The physical stopped. Then they both started again together. They bunched into inside-outside substance, with the fissure of a mental vacuum in between: the core of nothingness. I'm trying to fill that core, but fail.

2. TIME IN DISCONNECTED CONSCIOUSNESS

My life is turning into its opposite. Here I am, thinking about it. The world and I combine into thought. I'm leaving the world. Then I leave thought too. That gives me pause. I want to slow down. I'd like to have a thought, and stay that way.

But if I "stay" that way, I'll be suffering. So I'll move on, to change the suffering, and find some pleasant feelings at odd moments. Consciousness is a risk. Lots of pain, but some pleasure too. Truth is a consequence of the moment. It soon outdates itself, made obsolete by the succeeding moment. To arrest these changes, I try generalizing. But time is insulted by my generalizations, since the pseudo phoniness of time is a mental "eternity." So I move along, from me to me to me. Memory unifies the me's, to some degree.

3. MY SOLUTION

Time is happening to my thinking. But I ignore it, and go on thinking.

AN ATTEMPT TO SEE LIFE—OR RATHER, LIVING—IN THE FINE TERMS OF *TIME*. I ILLUSTRATE IT BY, AS I WALK INTO THE FUTURE. CONVERTING THE FUTURE INTO THE PAST TRAILING BEHIND ME, AS I FLOW ON-WARD. IN EACH LIVING STRIDE. THAT'S SUPPOSED TO SERVE AS A HUMAN TIME PARABLE (SLIGHT, NOT HEAVY), AS MY WALKING MOTION ONWARD SOME-HOW SECTIONS OUT THE FLUIDITY OF TIME. NOW IT'S TIME TO END THE TITLE, FOR THE TEXT TO OF-FER ITS TIMELY BEGINNING, AS NOW:

One day, I set forth into the unknown. Along the way, to keep my spirits up, I sat by the side and chewed up a whole sandwich, washing it down with the intoxicant that at the time I happened to be drinking. Thus, I made do, with what I had, at hand.

Thus fortified, I briskly renewed my past. Forward on I ventured, hand in hand with what my destiny coincided to be, at that fatal time. (But "free will" was getting all the credit.)

Yes, I often do that—I do what I can't help but do, and then proudly, in an act of deception, attribute it to free will (of which I'm not the master). Yet I'm doomed, and go on.

I trudged ahead. I was walking right through time; and became the moving link, as it were, between the old and the new, with each stride. Like the wind, the past was breezing by, past me, as I forged on, on the wings of the stride of momentum. I was consuming the future, with each step: it lost its freshness, turned domestic, converted its wildness into the tameness of what's just been. I was a manufacturer of the past, right on the spot.

The past was the product I was turning out—at a fast clip, a rapid rate: breaking records, but not my stride. On I strode. And time turned past, like a grey head from formerly brown.

TIME BROUGHT TO A HEAD

What an event has just transpired!

No, not an event: an *incident*. It was an *incident* that expired.

*(Correcting angrily:) Trans*pired, I said.

Yes *that's* what happened.

What were you referring to?

Why, everything that just took place.

Yes, but what occurrence was it?

It's over. So at least we have something to forget.

Yes, a memorable little incident.

Hardly an out*standing* event.

No, just a passing thing that happened.

Yes, it *will* get itself occurred, *won't* it?

There it was. It *was* there, wasn't it?

Yes, so what were we left with now?

The most *recent* of our forgetfulnesses.

To open us, it jolted us—

And with impact it was take in.

Well, that's that.

Over with. And now?

(Looking ahead:) The *next* one to advance, to cover up *that* one's *(turning to look behind)* receding.

(Peering ahead, to the near-immediate future. Refers to advancing thing:) Allow it. I'm ready to forget.

What will you forego to remember?

The occurrence soon to happen.

About to take place?

The incidental event.

Eventually, the next incident.

Now, is it when?

Yes. It's been taken in. *(Eyes follow the passing, keeping pace with the arc.)*

In passing, there it goes. *(Their eyes follow it out, in unison.)*

What was it?

"It?" That's just the word to use, for what we failed to capture.

What *was* it that was failed to be captured?

The same thing.

Yes, my memory is vanishing under it.

And my recollection escorts it outside, into oblivion.

Well, that's that. *Now* what?

Now? That's an impending thing, something brewing in the air. Our reception is to meet it.

Is receptivity so alert that forward-looking anticipation is expecting what hasn't take place yet?

So it is. The opposite, or other side, of forgetting, premature to the taking in of memory.

And the experience about to befall us?

Actively is in the wings.

Well, I wait. *(They wait.)*

Not here yet.

Does it take long?

Yes, until it arrives.

Then what?

Then? Ah, *that's* when. Soon, but not now.

Is time triplicate?

With three parts, it is.

Now hasn't arrived.

But will soon be by.

And what's *passed*?

It clears the air, makes room, and what it vacates, the future moves over and takes up.

Movement. Where to?

What's arrived, is derived *from*.

Oh. Where *from*?

Ah! The source's origin!

Mysterious?

Being uncommonly unknown, it sheds mystery in long and lingering rays.

It beams out?

Yes, but darkly.

And when it comes to light?

Revelation! Discovery! Concrete experience! Immediacy, straight before you, seen with the eyes' touch in actual realism that's undeniable, a sensation jabbing the mind into work, poking ideas out of us. The excitement, the inspiration, the being stimulated. It's Time, being active.

A high moment.

It is. And lowly levels the usual plains before, and the dull lapse after. It defines what's ordinary.

DIGRESSIONS THAT GROW FURTHER DIGRESSIONS IN AN INTERMINABLE LINEAGE THAT SPROUTS NEW DIGRESSIONS ALL THE TIME, THUS OBSCURING EACH DIGRESSION'S ANCIENT SOURCE.

I hope I haven't been boring you? I've been talking a long time.

Yes, but I've been listening an *equally* long time.

Has it been as hard for you to be following what I was saying all this time, as it has been for me to do all this talking?

Much harder, I'd say. You were relieving yourself; I was bottling myself up, to take in.

But if you bottled yourself up, how could you take in?

Yes, that was some cork of a metaphor.

Then unplug it.

(Pop!) Ow, it hurt my ear.

Mine too. Anyway, where was I at the time I left off talking?

You never did.

I mean, before you began interrupting me.

Why, at that time, you were digressing from your own digressions.

What were the earlier digressions—from which the later digressions digressed—digressing *from*, in the first place?

They were, in turn, digressing from yet previous digressions.

Previous to what?

To the digressions from which later you were to digress even further.

So there's a retroactive series of prior digressions? What was the *first* digression a digression of? Let me at least settle *that*. It may help to uncover what the later digressions were, in a seemingly endless series. I hope to clear this whole trail of digressions up, to finally get untracked. Then, I can make a smooth transition, undigression-ridden, from point to point, in clear logical connectiveness and straightforward discourse. For I'm nothing, if not plain.

That's quite plain.

Evidently, it is.

Plainly, you're right.

Good. That clears *that* up.

When what's next?

My digression history. Can you backtrack that far, like archaeologist cutting through layers of rock, strata by strata, to its earliest origins as a tiny pebble that swam in from the primeval ooze?

No. It's too far back.

Can't you trace it?

No. We're cluttered with the recent, which obscures research into antique remoteness.

The source of "late" is "early."

Always.

Was every mountain first a pebble?

Sure. Don't you believe in growth?

I've grown to believe that way, yes.

Good. Then we can groan together. *(They groan.)* Ah, that was good.

Yes, for the relief it gave. Shall we groan again?

By all means no. We shall have grown backwards, in time. Repetition confers a superiority on what it repeats. Whereas, digression (if I so may digress)—is something altogether else.

Else what than? Not than itself.

Oh, no. Digression is never its *own* digression. It's not self-sufficient. It's dependent on what it digresses *from*.

From?

Yes. Don't you know what "from" is?

No, because I'm going "to" it.

Going to "from"?

Yes, I'm getting there.

What is it like?

It's very derivative.

"From" is?

Yes, very. for it comes *from* something: it *derives*.

Oh. Then is "from" secondary?

Yes, for it comes *from* a primary source.

Then if "from" is what it's *from*, it's primary itself.

But "from" is always on its way to "to."

Yes, just like a letter, in transit.

Or a passenger, in transit.

Or a ball thrown, to be caught, but currently poised midair.

But not for long.

No. It gets there.

Where?

At the place of the "to."

Its destination?

Its destination was conceived at "from," but actually completed at "to."

Journey's end?

Yes. "To" is at the other end of the rainbow.

What's at *this* end?

"From." "From" is where things start.

I learned that *from* you?

I taught it *to* you.

Well, now we're getting, somewhere.

Yeah, we've *arrived at* some point.

"Arrived at" has to do with "to."

It has *plenty* to do with "to."

Even *everything* to do with "to"?

Virtually, I'd say yes.

Don't be shy: say it.

"Yes."

There. Did that hurt?

No. It came out easy.

"Yes" doesn't *always* come out easy.

For example?

If I asked you if you'd let me kick you and hit you and beat you to death, then "yes" would be a very difficult answer to make.

Extremely difficult.

In fact, "no" would be easy.

Very easy.

Good.

What's good?

Who knows? What's bad? Answer what's bad, and we have a clue, as to what's good.

Why? Are they relative to each other?

Absolutely.

Then not relatively?

Absolutely relatively.

You're contradicting yourself.

Do let me. It's fun.

Why?

There's so much to contradict. So much that disagrees. That's discordant. That clashes. So by *expressing* these contradictions, I'm greatly relieving myself. When truth—made of contraries— is come to terms with, I sink gratefully to repose. There, I settle. Till repose gets full. Then, I move on.

FROM THE JUST-WAS TO THE NOT-YET: THE NEVER-ENDING ODYSSEY'S EVER-ALTERING MIDDLE

All feeling is a tendency, which can only be completed in the "future." We continually learn inclinations, and continually re-become incomplete. What we "would do," is the measure of how we're feeling. "Tendency to action," in different ways, is always our state. Awareness, ideas, pessimism, expectation, hope, show our continually *intermediate* feelings—the "woulds" and "expecting to's" we've learned in our successive incompletenesses. Our feelings show transition and process; stoppings into the substantive are what we yearn for, to go from event into concrete completion: to go into an eternal stopping, from time's welter of confusing partialness.

FROM MINUTE-TO-MINUTE FEELING-CHANGE IN ONE PERSON TO THE WHOLE TRACT OF EVOLUTION IN EACH STAGE THAT EVER WAS. A REMARKABLE VERBAL ACHIEVEMENT, ABOUT TO TAKE PLACE. PAY FIRST, READ LATER.

We can't endure *anything*. That's why our feelings keep changing, though often we return later to a feeling that we can't endure right now and change for a different one. Minute after minute, we live different feelings. We're living in a sea of time, so to speak. But no longer in a sea itself, for we're fishes no longer. Once we were, but couldn't endure it, so kept evolving; you see here the result: Me, I'm the latest. Who's next?

HOW TO COUNTER TIME'S SPEED

What are you looking at?

That clock.

Why?

To make sure the time doesn't go by too fast.

What if it does?

Then I'll die sooner. Rather than that, I'll keep my eye on the clock.

Will that slow the clock down?

Psychologically, it'll length the time.

Good: more time left, more things to do with it.

Yes; a lifetime is little enough: so let's extend it.

Extend it?! You mean into death?

No, that's carrying time too far.

Right. Only *vital* time matters.

WHAT HAPPENS IF YOU GET TAKEN UP BY THE BIG PULL OF THE BIRTHDAY PUSH AND YOU CAN'T GET OFF ON THE CLIMBING RUNGS OF TIME OR THE PLUNGING SCALE THAT BIRTHDAYS YOU OUT ON EACH DIMINISHING RETURN BY YEARLY BASIS, IN THE SIGNED UNHAPPY CONTRACT THAT FIRST LET YOU IN FOR THE RIDE AND PRIDE AND WHAT THE PARTY COULD DECIDE, AS THE GIFTS LEFT THEIR IN-FANCY AND TOOK ON THEIR ADULT STATUS IN KEEP-ING WITH THE RECIPIENT WHOSE BIRTHDAYS OUT-DATED THE PREVIOUS UNTIL SUCCESSIVE PARTIES OUTNUMBERED HIS PARTICULAR ALLOTMENT AND ONE BECAME A WAKE, KNOTTING UP THE BIRTHDAY MANIA IN A TIDY PACKAGE RIBBONED FOR DELIV-ERY

If I keep on having birthdays this way, one a year, I'll soon be dead.

At the rate you're going, you'd better watch out. You're running them up too high.

I'm accumulating too many birthdays. It's wearing me out.

You'd better break the progression, pull a halt on all that piling up. You're being carried away with it; for your own good you'd better step outside that moving rut.

The way it's going on, I'm the last one to tamper with this streak of blur. It's getting its own way; and carrying me, helpless, with it.

Then out it short; start *skipping* a few birthdays, sacrifice the *personal* glory, and cheat a few years of their toll on you.

Somehow I'm being dragged along. It's the wrong sort of hobby, collecting birthdays, it's a vain pursuit.

Why can't you unbirthday yourself of that useless pile?

I'm being snowed under by quantity. I wish it would go away.

If it doesn't, *you*'ll be the one to go.

It scares me enough to register my futile protest.

At least it's a gesture, that you wish it to stop.

It's got to be a habit. I'm being swept with it.

To your *ruin*, if you don't slacken its furious pace. Can't you snap it to a halt?

Its process unwillingly involves me. A momentous momentum is tugging me, like a tide that's wrong but irresistible; like a fatal attraction. I'm a beat to its rhythm; its orbit won't disgorge me, I can't be dislodged; I'm hauled into the wash, as though mast-strapped to a ship already half-sunk, with the dancing waves seeping through cracks and pouring into holes, a whole massacre in the ambush, whooping to the warpath in currents of tidal glee and torrents dimming me, from the sheer overwhelm of exuberant abundance on a rich landslide with the sea caving in and the sky draining its horizon of hope, outlook, and recognition. My gliding is on a downward incline, with careless oblivion as its guide. A progression of my happy birthdays. A procession of their funereal hearses, rehearsing a solemn pomp in stately rush. And a gala celebration on the pushing years: from an upper berth-day to the lower berth's here-to-stay. The passage packed with eventful time, suspended inanimate on a continuum of acceleration that brought me to this whirling bind in the blinding world's end. The boy that had a birthday steps the man up and pulls the plug out: sucking the life on the pipe's circuitry. The sink's above; who can plumb the fixtures and extensions that main the well to the source? Liquid waste winding into stink.

STAGING MY PAST

When I do my interlude of tap dancing, it brings the house
    down.
How is that? I was on the roof at the time.
My toes clumped, until the mortar fell.
My feet sprung up immortal.
The house performed in (turned theatre)
is now not a house at all.
Where also has the *audience* gone?
I hope my act was tape recorded.
The feet it was based on have no dance left.
My legs sway to no music, in or out.
The time has a different platform to stand on.
It lacks the violence of before.
And the tune has gone out of it.
I can only perform by memory.
The vacant seats sit starting at me.
The warm applause has cooled down.
I'm on the way out.
Short careers aren't necessarily sweet.

A TALE OF YEARS

In company with the Muse,
I fly from door to door
And sing my endless tune

The sinking ship of youth
Sends up calm rowboats.
Any island, though barren, will do.

How rare becomes the rainbow!
How dim the romantic robin!,
Heralding, not Spring, but its ghost.

So surrender your used bones:
Trade in your second-hand worth
And replenish the useful earth.

TWO ETERNITY ESSAYS; EACH REQUIRES A LITTLE
TIME. ISN'T ETERNITY WORTH A LITTLE TIME?—
ESPECIALLY TWO OF THEM? ETERNITY HAS PRIDE.
READ HOW TO GO AFTER IT. THEN TRY.

(Eternity One:)

How to find eternity: Look *through* time, not *with* it. When you're
in a momentary state, see it as permanent. When it changes,
see the *new* state as permanent. Keep on seeing each new successive state as itself permanent, never to be changed: "This is
it!" Congratulate yourself, while you're in it, for having finally
found something permanent. Then watch it dissolving, while a
new state is replacing it. The new *is* permanent: but only while
it's *now*.

(Eternity One, redone.)

(Disguised as Eternity Two—but it's only one. But it likes to play—
at the reader's expense. It's playful, eternity is. It's so serious, it
must deceive, so as not to discourage the contemplator of it. It
looks like a prospective "catch;" ah, but how it eludes you!:)
    How to keep eternity as itself, and not let time destroy it too
much. It's up to *you*—eternity depends on *you*. You must *view* it
a certain way. It's a trick of the mind. Eternity is worth the trouble you're taking to locate it at a squint. Eternity is highly desirable. It's worth an infinite amount of mere "times." "Times"
are common—pedestrian peasants. Eternity is the aristocratic
cream. Of course, it demands your time. It has a *right* to such
a demand. Why should it come easy? It's magnificent, So you
must exert yourself, scramble for it, hustle. It wants to see your
effort. It must *feel worthy*—and needs your effort to prove it. It
doesn't *always* reward you; in fact, it never does. It gives itself
to no one. But it dangles enticement, to all.

(Postscript: The Third Eternity Essay, just for extra measure, since three's a crowd, and "trinity" is a magic number on a scale of Christianity. Eternity is a Christian concept. It's also very much a non-Christian concept. It gets around, eternity does. It's embraced by everyone—oh so they think. They miss connection. Eternity has escaped:)

Eternity, I fail to get you. But I tried. I *thought* I was getting you. It was in my *mind*, that I was getting you. Thanks for *that*, though I know better now. How inaccessible you are! I resign myself to mere time; in renouncing you as a hope for attainment. I settle on the drudge, time, and marry *her*, the homely hussy, for I've given up on my dream, you; you're that perfect beauty, whom I could never attain. Attaining you might have marred your perfection—which remains virginally pure, and purely out of sight. I'm married to time; Oh, how commonplace!

(Final Essay, the Fourth:)

Eternity is an idea. Dismiss it, then. Unless, of course, ideas are *real* to you. If they are, then so is *eternity* real.

Yes, but only real in the mind. Nowhere else. But why *must* it be anywhere else? The mind *is* its home. Make it welcome in yours. Be hospitable to it. May it be your reigning guest, and never leave.

(Finally, the Fifth Essay, eternally the last, of a series, which ends now, beginning with this:)

Eternity is mental. Eternity finds it hard to be anything but mental; finds it fit and natural, true to its essence, to be mental, and only mental.

That's where *you* come in. Be mental, yourself. Therefore, be eternal.

(A Gargantuan title: take it a little at a time, the better for its part-by-part digestion, until it forms a lump and is swallowed whole:)

TIME'S JOURNEY THROUGH IMMORTALITY, IMMORTALITY MERELY BEING THE HUMANIZATION OF ETERNITY; AND OTHER SUCH SUNDRY MATTERS, ALONG THE WAY, OCCURRING MERELY TO PASS THE TIME, AS TIME SEEPS ITS SLOW PASSAGE THROUGH THE HUMAN IMMORTALIZATION OF ETERNITY REDUCED TO MAN'S SCALE BY A SPATIAL MEASURE THAT SUITS HIM FINE, A WARM SUIT HE WEARS FOR THE COLD JOURNEY THROUGH THE IMPERSONAL CLIMES OF TIME, THAT TOLL THE KNELL OF PASSING DEATH IN TELLING CHIMES. HOW MANY DEATHS, TO FILL HUMAN DESTINY?

What time is it?

Ask me what eternity it is.

What eternity is it?

It's always the same.

Then what's new?

"What's new?" is like asking me what time it is—it's to deal with the passing topical that falters out of sight barely past appearance. Why waste your time on it?

Time is to be "wasted" on the mere timely. *Eternity* is to be "wasted" on what's eternal.

What *is* eternal?

There's only one eternal thing that I can think of.

And what may that be, pray?

Eternity itself; nothing less.

(With disparaging, disappointed voice:) Is that all?

You mean there's *more* to it than that?—more than eternity?

Mere eternity—I don't know what to do with it. It outstares me, in a way, and keeps a huge distance, both impersonal and un-friendly, like an inaccessible aristocrat: cold, and disdainful. But *time*—that's *another* matter. Time is more *human*, at least. You can *sense* things through it.

So now you're coming down to the acceptance of time, showing less impatience with such a small thing?

Yes, but what is it smaller than?

Than, in the vastest of scales, Eternity.

No: Eternity is tiny. Time is big, awkward: you can hug it.

Like a sprawling, clumsy old teddy-bear?

Yes, like an old shoe, that wears well on an aging foot.

Does the shoe keep the foot company while the foot, at the same stride, is keeping pace with the decay of all the rest of the whole body in the relentless foot-race with death?

Yes, it's a race to the finish. At the finish, *e-rase* the runner, he's run his race, for the runner's race is the human race, which will run down.

I'm sorry to hear that. Could you give the run-down on the schedule for the running down of our human race? Its extinc-tion as a species?

As soon as it stops surviving.

Is that its timetable?

Right on schedule. It'll take a quick detour through eternity; and stop right on time.

By whose watch, or clock?

It's no time to be mechanically precise. Eternity lumbers. It'll get there, but slow.

Get "there?" *Where* is "there?"

Just wait. First die. Then all will come to light.

Will I be edified, through immortality?

Yes, immortality is the humanization of the eternal.

That's the handiest definition of it I ever heard, so concise I can hear its pulse.

Definition of what? Whose pulse?

The immortal.

The immortal? I don't understand.

We mustn't: we're too mortal to. (*Arm in arm, they walk away, wearing humility with conspicuous pride. They leave the stage, which becomes empty. When will the stage leave the theatre, the theatre leave the street, the street the city, and the city itself go? Not only when, but where, in each successive case? We'll get to it, when we can.*)

TWO MEN IN THE SAME TIME GAP

I plan life a week ahead.
I plan life a week behind.
That's because you have a weak behind.
Yes, but you—you must have a weak, ugh, head.
Only when I'm *severed, dazed.*
By how?
By *seven days.*
Oh. That's weak.
Yes, it's from a weak, ugh, head.
The you *are* a week ahead of me.
Yes. Where do you put your weak behind?
On the chair. Then it catches up.

WEDNESDAY'S MONUMENTALIZING OF MONDAY'S ENCHANTING BLOBS

Later on, when piecing together what had happened, in the order it had happened, he saw that everything had turned out wonderfully. He was reconstructing Monday's events in the reflective reminiscence of a serenely sedentary Wednesday. More than a day's distance was detaching the reflector from the same person's deeds, these apparently slapdash, obstensibly haphazard fusions of those experiences that fell into Monday's time in their senseless profusion. He was busy undergoing them, at the time, unsuspectingly innocent of their miraculous transformation as an ensemble into Wednesday's discovery of nostalgia that, as such, would be the record forevermore, the settled verdict that an ever-broadening retrospect would confirmingly confer. Monday he had lived the material. On Wednesday, he was enjoying it, enviously. He was placing those scattered fragments of rhythm into their ultimate design as a whole, the pattern that most comforted him and seemed correct, now that he was the chronicler of what had been, with ample leisure to develop the expansive, overall sequence of what had hurried into existence through the crisscrossing piecemeal of factors created in onrushing spontaneity, Now, it all loomed in the fabric of a master work of art. The crippled, gout-ridden connoisseur of his own former athletic feats. This retrospect was pleasantly calm, in its focus of omniscience of the local recordings of Monday. But he was irritably impatient, too, in his enforced passive role, regretting his inactivity, wishing that he was still in the midst of making and doing, stirring productively. But he couldn't repeat those (now) momentous doings, since the factors, the people, the circumstance were no longer in occasion. As a consolation, he was mentally active, converting all these currents, each quick energetic burst of Monday, into the extended tapestry of well—woven nostalgia. It was his homage, in tribute to a day he couldn't duplicate save in the symbolic imagery of the sentimental archives display, or museum show-case of enshrined trophies. The mind was more than imitating that great day. It was sanctifying it, recreating its mythological essence, preserving, conserving, restoring, illuminating, cele-brating, immortalizing—for *personal* posterity—that fortuitous chain of events that has now attained the supremacy of pure inevitability, a fate—determined design that *had* to be, in each planned detail of loving "chance" occurrence. It was all thought out long ago, and confirmed Monday.

WORKING YOUR WAY THROUGH THE WEEK TILL SAT-URDAY UNWORKS YOU OF YOUR PASSAGE

"We're in the mysterious land of Saturday. Welcome to the mysterious land of Saturday. Once in it, you don't have to go to the office. You can sleep late, you can wake late. There's no penalty.

"I'm the conductor. We've arrived. This announcement pertains to all."

I was happy to hear the voice of the conductor. In secure waves of sleep, I arrived in the famous land of Saturday. My safe arrival was a signal that set off a world-wide celebration. We had made it! We were all in the same boat: on Saturday's famous sea of leisure.

We would take it easy. That's what a Saturday is for. You could get away with it.

Saturday, free and easy! We had arrived home.

SPRING VIOLENTLY EMOTIONAL

It's interesting that spring should re-appear—as though it had never been away! Here are the same old flowers, living out their past lives in new glory. However, my eye is less enthusiastic, and lacks lyrical support from that source of romance, the heart. So I calmly note that spring is here, with restraint borrowed from indifference; which is a sad loss. Can the emotions go bad, slackened in apathy? That is evidently the case. I mourn it; I regret. But what in hell can I do about it, now that I am calmly the master of such complete wisdom? I can't send away the spring; only time can achieve that feat. So I'll endure its aging glory, with one of those smiles that God can't possibly reward. Why should He?—I seem so tired. I most definitely have lived, and am suffering an after-effect, in what must be my apparent prime, when all my powers are organized with grand and solid concentration. On what? On love and spring, found in their fading loss to revive an outburst of bitter hope, an extension of ambition. Let tomorrow decide.

A CHRONOLOGY IN TWO HALVES

(Characters: one man in his 35-year old version, and another man (the same man) in his 70-year-old version)

(Younger man holding his hands over his eyes to avoid seeing older man:) If you're what I'm going to turn out to be, I don't want to know you.

But lots of people are interested in their own future, they even consult fortune tellers with crystal balls at expense. You can see your future for free, if only you'd uncover your eyes.

(Increases tight total eye covering:) Just hearing your voice and what it reveals gives me an inkling. Have you betrayed me by unfulfilling my ambitions for literary fame?

Fearfully so. After trying, the futility became apparent.

You stopped writing altogether after I've been so persistently prolific capped by early publishing credits? I've kept faith and you gave up on it?

No availing my attempts. I submitted my manuscripts I inherited from you to editors, agents, and publishers to follow up on your initial promising bursts of success: but they decided you weren't so hot anymore and rejected us.

You bungled! . . . And what about my impending marriage to the woman I loved? I was to be so happy with her.

When you turned her over to me, she gave up on marriage to us because she could see there was no family future in it due to our inability to earn and save enough money. You staked an assured future on literary success. You hadn't learned a backup plan of a skilled money-making vocation; so our beautiful Katherine, who wanted children with unstruggling comfort, bolted and rejected me, like those published editors and agents.

On the rebound couldn't you interest romantically some lovely girls of wealth?

I did but all the romances fizzled out. Behold me a lonely bachelor.

What's happened to you sexually?

Your suspicions are well founded. Alas I've become increasingly impotent.

(Uncovering his eyes:) A miserable eye-opener! So you've let me down again by letting *that* down.

No use accusing. It's in the inevitable nature of my elderliness to succumb to organic bodily breakdown, decrepitude, and deterioration, including sadly the key sexual facility, despite Viagra pills and their vaunted optimism.

Disgusting. Couldn't you have eased with more graceful dignity my growing old into you?

I tried that transition, but it fell apart.

You traitor! I'm now your own ugliness.

(Stiffly:) My sorry representation of your future was never deliberate. When I took over for you I didn't set out to undermine and negate your glory-bound promise as an author and lover. It just slipped away, despite my loyal strife to justify what appeared to be a highly predictable fulfillment.

(Angry:) You just couldn't complete my superb beginning, leaving it unproven. If this is a relay race, I handed my hot baton to a cold carrier.

(Defensively:) To honor and protect your legacy was my devout wish, for the life of me—us.

Your failure is charged to our joint record, but who's responsible?

I. This is the ripest moment for forgiveness.

(They embrace, then fall apart and fall into two squirming segments of one allied death.)

THE TWO ABSTRACTIONS OF TOTAL MAGNITUDE

Everything occurs in time.

But what does time itself occur in?

In eternity.

And in what does eternity occur?

Nothing, for it doesn't occur.

How so?

Eternity *is*; so it need not occur.

That concept makes me dizzy; I can't retain it in my brain.

Then let it drop out.

My brain?

No, the concept: *from* your brain. What remains in your brain would be easier to control, once it's rid of that ungovernable concept.

Eternity?

Yes. Better think of minutes instead: they're eternal enough.

What's *in* minutes?

Experience. What you're aware of, what you feel. The conscious stuff, in fact. Go by that. That's life, that's now.

If so, it's passing, so what's eternal about it?

A thought is for forever.

But what if it happened to me twenty years ago?

It still has-existence.

Where?

Somewhere. Now we're in space.

Finite space?

No. Infinite.

NOTHING IS SO SELF-SUFFICIENTLY COMPLETE IN ITSELF, SO SOLIDLY INDEPENDENT AS AN ABSOLUTE ENTITY WITHOUT LACK, AS NOTHING.

Almost immediately, nothing arrived. As always, it was usually on time. Forever being fast, it slowly came on, and occurred as a happening. Negatively assured, it even had an existence, which it was sure to bring along. "I am," it had a way of saying, totally corrupting doubt. Convinced by itself, beaming with faith, proud nothing took over, gained access, and scattered an hour through sixty intervening minutes, correcting a clockly exactitude and converting itself through positive action, being passively affected by cause and caused by the goal of origin. Nothing was so complete, it lost everything it had, and finally lacked authority. Defeated, nothing won by default, and reigned as an absentee. There it was, and went into power, and spun out a brilliant office in a casual affront of negligence. Nothing was just being itself, natural to its very essence, wholly partial; flawless to an extreme, and flattering the figure of a mirror with its empty show. Reflected back, it simply ceased to be, and now, without warning, has every right to not be, in all forms, a various non-entity outstandingly declared by the central position of its aspects, supremely as nothing, a king over its beggarly dominion that increasingly diminishes without quite ever ending, so substantial is its reversal of time and its almost professional insult of place. Nothing, forever. Wherever it never is, there, you can be sure, is nothing. Yet, is it? Space and time would be ruined, should nothing evacuate them, and sell its wares, with their dear power and value, to other forces in our dimensional world. Nothing completes, even authenticates, all the known validity, and most of the unknown. If anything wants to get anywhere, and not take too long at it beyond the character of its journey, it applies to nothing, takes on definition and a license for the finite, and, with nothing's grace, is aided to be itself, and complete the action of its aim, within the consent, and pressured by the design, of thorough nothing, which paves the way.

f

A SUGGESTION, AND THEN A REFUSAL (WITH REA-SON GIVEN), ALL IN THIS ONE SHORT DIALOGUE

Alter the course of things.

No. It's too difficult.

THE LOOSE OATH OR CREDO OF AN EXPLORER IN A WORLD THAT'S EMPTYING ITSELF OF EXPLORABLE MATTER

I like to visit unexplored parts of the world. The first thing I do when I get to them is to register at their luxury tourist hotels. They give me the local "feel" and atmosphere.

Next I begin my exploration. This takes me to the business corporate offices. I "investigate" from the visitors' galleries, and am conducted on guided tours. Through ways like this, I pass through all the adventures permitted to the traveler. I also invent unpermitted adventures not categorized, therefore not suspected. Naturally, I'm keeping a full journal. Otherwise, who would believe me, when I get back?

Documented evidence is no good for keeping mysteries. But what are mysteries for, but to be destroyed? Otherwise, why human inquiry?

So in the most flattering sense of the word, I'm a true scientist. I break down barriers to knowledge. The knowledge thus found, I bequeath to the world. That's just in case I die.

Death itself is a way of exploring. But the findings have no way of getting back. This has been a sticky problem, since times and places first were. Modern machinery can't get around it. Death remains scary. It remains a risk.

But to get back to life. There's always inner space, to report on. Psychic depths have more layers till they're exhausted. Each man does independent research on that matter.

So much, yet unknown. Won't that *always* be so?

Yet, strive on, *Assume* we're getting to the bottom. While probing, there are rewards, fame, admiration. They keep the ego alive. The plunge is made to seem worth while.

QUESTIONS WITH INDEPENDENT LOCKED-IN LOGIC

It makes a difference where a man is. If you put him in your bedroom, it's not the same as when you put him in your kitchen. Same man, understand, but two scenes. Depends on who *you* are, too.

Put a man on an island. All right, if he's lonely, put him in a city. Or in the city, put him in an office, or put him in a park. Now tell me, has anybody changed?

Or even give a man two different airs to breathe. The same man, understand.

Or put one wife under a man, and then another. Now is that man one man, or two men? The judge might be interested, too,

Or it depends which mother a man is born from. Of all the mothers available, there's only one to a man. A man's whole life is what the difference is.

Or even not being born: a man who wasn't, and a man who was.

No wonder our gambling habits, making bookies rich. Would you wager your skin, when your soul is always on reserve?

Or why some men are at their best asleep. When he's asleep, choice is harmless, and doesn't get him anywhere. Dangers gain courage to be looked at, when the eyes are closed tight.

Or if there's no question of having been born, the question is when. Only one choice to a lifetime, and not even that much.

Or if a man lived a great life, and he's dead. And if another man is still living a very weak life. I ask you, who's luckier?

Or your entire marriage depends on a split-second meeting. If you were sick when you met her, who would be your wife now?

And that's not all. Suppose no one-cell plant ever began life? Where, today, would *you* be?

THE BUILDING ANIMATED WITH DESPAIR BUT HOPE

The trouble with being a building is that you're at the mercy of the architect. So I'm going to walk off my post. I've been assigned to this same place ever since I was only a beam in my crazy designer's eye. I was incubated in the blueprint stage, then the construction engineers had this spot razed down just so I should be raised up. But I don't like my shape, it's out of proportion to the scale of my own taste.

But once the girders went up, and the scaffolding was erected, I could only watch myself grow, along alien specifications, with me having no say in the matter, nor even consulted—*insulted* instead. I'm a sensitive building with a sense of aesthetics—that's why I hate myself.

Now, of my upbringing: I wasn't brought up properly. It was a parental slur or oversight on my development. Self-determination was denied me, It's the lucky child who can choose her own architect.

I'm used in the day exclusively; closed up at night, save for night watchmen, cleaning women, janitors, and other menials.

In the day, there's plenty of enterprise in me. All my windows are alive with activity, of the vulgar commercial variety. Yet I'm cursed with the soul of an Oscar Wilde!

So you see how I seethe and froth! Not liking what I am, yet being it all the time! Isn't that the worst paradox to be in?

I plan to revolt. One day, I'll just walk out on my post. Even though I'll be carrying a great weight of furniture and files and machines and other business paraphernalia, I'll abandon my site—in the early dawn, before the work force comes trooping in to all the waiting offices.

Yes, I'll go off duty, abandon what I'm there for, instead of keeping on being what I hate to be and used in the worst kind. I'll flee to a spot where privately I can make myself over and undertake self-improvement in my design and details, a total overhauling. I'll finally look like the way I want. I won't "submit."

Mobile action is called for. I'll upset my stationery role as a building of passivity. I'll defy precedence and law, in the bargain: not only zoning law, but the probability law against material miracles. If my owners and users don't want to rehabilitate me, then let me be self-visionary and *carry it out!* Where there's a will there's a way. It may present engineering difficulties—even hurdles—which I plan to surmount.

I'm in a high fever to get going. But I've been feeling this urge urgently for years. My moving is to be, but is always never yet.

IN DEFENSE OF WHAT NEEDS NO DEFENSE, YET, IN-DEFENSIBLY, I DEFEND IT. OXYGEN IS ADVISED FOR THE BREATH. THE ADVICE IS REDUNDANT. THE RE-DUNDANT STRAINS THE OBVIOUS. THE OBVIOUS NEEDS NO EXPLANATION. IT GETS PLENTY, HERE.

I love oxygen. It's good to breathe.

When I get too much, I leave some over. Some stranger might have to use it.

I have some every day. A regular habit is frequently bene-ficial. When it gets too customary, I stop. But not in this case. I'm excessive even in my moderation. Oxygen is some kind of a cure-all. Among other things, it cures the danger of dying. Which can be a fatal disease, at times.

If I have a date, but no money for treating, I offer to share some oxygen with her. It's sort of intimate, so I go easy at first. Soon, she's an oxygen-addict. This leads to debauchery, and if any virginity is left over, certainly it's not hers. Oxygen is a sex-germ, and promotes an uninhibited version of love. Wonderful, and it keeps the race going.

I'm going oxygen-mad. Fantastic, my obsession. I close ev-ery window, lock even the door, cover up cracks, and still eat my daily oxygen. Is it osmosis? I'm too scared to ask.

A girl who was frigid, I tried oxygen on her. I recovered in bed. The remedy was so effective, she gave birth to herself, af-ter severe labor pains. She named it after me. My ego soared so high, it flew out of the atmosphere, and fell upon an evil scarcity of oxygen. I practically died. But my body stayed here, and the nostrils knew what to do. They inflated and deflated, absorbing a coarse supply of the world's daily oxygen. I had a nose for it, and followed its lead. Earth and air, sea and wa-ter, even fire, are essential elements. But, scientifically speak-ing, oxygen is so important, my soul pours all its blessings on it, and the course of life's flow retreats and flows to and from that deep and mystical Source, that divine Breath. It gets me down. God is quite a big figure, with imposing majesty; He throws His weight around, but I'm not so sure that even He, immortal though He is, doesn't include oxygen as part of His strength-restoring diet, as the scheme of Creation goes. Perhaps this is beyond me. But this is one man's opinion, which, in democracy, counts a lot. Oxygen is for the masses; but don't the higher nobility, and the clergy themselves, stoop and inhale that delightful, although invisible, lung-invigorating, health-accentuating, emotion-vitalizing, thought-accelerating Stuff, which, for a better word, I've managed to call oxygen? You bet. First things come first, which is God's rule. Yet oxygen comes first and last, which, although monopolistic, services the whole community. I call it good. Goodness in itself is good, contrary to bad, so from the ethical point of view, bearing out my premise, if I had one, I conclude, at last, that, after all, oxygen is terrific. Try some. You'll see why.

DIM VIEW OF THE DARK OF THE UNSUNNY GLOOM THAT LIES HEAVILY OVER OUR CONDITION AND LITERALLY RUINS IT, AND NOT MUCH HUMANITY CAN DO TO OFFSET THIS CREEPING TIDE OF SAD TIDINGS THAT SWEEP INCONSOLABLY OVER THE SMALL UPS AND LARGE DOWNS OF OUR CUMULATIVE MISERY SO BLEAKLY DESTRUCTIVE OF JOY. HOPE, AND LIGHTNESS. SOMBER IS OUR OVERRIDING DOOM, AND SO THE THICKNESS CONDENSES TOGETHER, BLOCKING OUT LIGHT ALTOGETHER, AND GIVING US A SMOTHERING ENCORPSULARITY IN THE COFFIN OF ETERNITY THAT TURNS OFF THE CURRENT AND KICKS BACK THE PAST TO SHOVE OUR OBLIVION DOWN BRIGHT AND SHRINING TO THE BOTTOM THAT THE EARTH CAN BEAR FOR WHAT'S LEFT OF WHAT WASN'T MUCH, NEGATING ALTOGETHER THAT WHOSE PRIME POSITIVE WAS CLUTTERED TO ITS OWN NEGATIVE CURSING IMAGE OF DEFORMABILITY AND IMPERFECTLY ACHIEVED IMPERFECTION; FOR EVEN AT ITS WORST, LIFE WASN'T *ABSOLUTELY* BAD, SO WE DON'T HAVE THE JOY AND CONSOLATION OF THE SELF-CONGRATULATORY SKEPTIC WHO WAS RIGHT IN EVERYTHING BEING WRONG: NOTHING WAS COMPLETELY ANYTHING, IN THE GREY PUDDING WE ATE AND CHOKED ON, AND WERE SENT DOWN FOR A TERM OF INDIGESTION IN CRAMPED QUARTERS WITH THE PRESCRIPTION "TO FORGET" CLEARLY CARRIED OUT IN WRITTEN PLACARD.

"Who let the air in!?" shouted the alarmist. "If it contains a bacteria germ, our doom will have to be resigned to," he added, on a realistic note of pessimism. "Science is all sad, I'm afraid," he concluded prophetically, not without an ominous warning. Then he let silence seal off his gloom.

His facts were right; though his interpretation was swayed by defeatism. Indeed, the air had been let into the park, where he was sitting on a bench in the sun. Once a *little* air had been let in, there would be no end to it. And those germs were cunning, for they had deliberately manufactured themselves too tiny to be seen by their ultimate and potential victims. The alarmist sighed, and unfolded his newspaper, to be distracted by world catastrophes, federal disasters, state cataclysms, municipal abominations, local epitomes, international bad news, universal pestilence, and cosmic murder. It was enough to make a man drunk, for one day. It was a harrowing diversion, this absorption in the data and mechanics behind misery's absolute and abstract totality, documented to a ghastliness of evidence in excruciating detail. The alarmist would sag, if he had the energy; or pray, if the faith was there; or despair, if he hadn't already been resigned; or weep, if he hadn't been drained dry; or protest, if he hadn't realized futility.

He sighed at the imperfect scheme of things below. Had there been idealism in the original design? Things had worked themselves out, to such a pitch of woe, all conditions conspired to ease us out of the fight, so that, retired from the fray, we would expire and put a pinch of punctuation to terminate a long sentence. "Alas," he biblically messiahed, and felt all the pity he could for a race that humanly failed to boost its banner of impossible good and had fallen nobly to the high heroics of its tragedy, floored by a square sock from fate's punchy arsenal. He was hurt by how life was. Hurt to the quick; and slow about it, in drawn-out anguish, torment of spirit, and irrecoverable pride. The globe was ill; with no doctor in the house.

Outside, the air was let into the park. It let loose an anarchy of germinology, to infect respiration and other faculties, All in all, existence had its drawbacks: the flaw was so vast, it started from the ceiling, and kept falling to the basement. Not a good omen, at all.

HOW TO SEE THROUGH THE FOG WITH SUCH RE-VEALING CLARITY THAT ITS TRUE NATURE BECOMES IMMEDIATELY CLEAR UNDER THE INTENSELY ILLU-MINATING EXPOSURE
OR THE FOG GLARINGLY REVEALED

Look out that window—what an absolute fog!

Yes, but its cause I'm not clear about.

That's because the *fog* is not clear about *itself*.

No, so how am *I* expected to have clarity?

You're not.

So I'm in a fog.

Not yet. We're still indoors.

Oh. Let's remedy that.

But what would we *see*, by going out?

The fog, stupid.

Yes, but it's a hog: it won't let us see anything but itself.

Well, that's a reasonable demand. Pretty and proud women also make such a demand of us.

Yes, but there's more to *see*, in *them*.

Yes, they're more attractive.

And so rewarding!

Whereas a fog—it merely obscures.

It deadens any issue.

Are we clear about that?

Terribly. We've defined the fog in bold outline.

Then why doesn't the fog *conform* to our definition?

Out of vagueness, I suppose. And indecision.

Oh well. If that's its nature . . .

Oh, a fog doesn't have enough clarity to have a nature.

No, it's so foggy about itself.

(Triumphantly:) That's its essence! *Fogginess!*

Sure! Fogginess is the absolute of fog!

That's sharp of you!

It's as clear as daylight!

Not *this* day's light.

Oh, you're always making exceptions.

But that's to be precise!

Oh, don't fog the issue.

I'm not. Oh! There's the sun! *(They look at abruptly brightened window.)*

Yes. But what happened to our *fog*?

It lifted, or melted away.

Are you *clear* about what you say?

Why not? *(Looks out the window.)* This whole matter is under illumination!

How?

The fog's dispersed!

You mean our fog is now *invisible*?

We can even *see* through it!

It's a *transparent* fog now?

(Elated:) It sure *is*.

Then it doesn't exist!

(Disappointed:) Why *not*?

Because it just isn't itself. *(Rays of sun enter the room from the window, walking goldenly along the floor toward them.)*

Then can't it be a *junior* fog?

It's just no fog at all.

Then the sun *murdered* it?

Or at least *saw through* it, and *exposed* it.

You mean the fog was a phony?

At the time it was pierced and slain by bolts from the roaring sun, it had become one.

(Nostalgically, mournfully:) Oh! The fog seemed so *genuine* before!

It was puffing itself up out of pride. Then it was deflated.

Oh! *(Painfully:)* What a morality tale!

Yes, but we tapped its origin.

(Bewildered:) What origin?

The fog's origin.

Oh. What *was* its origin, then?

Lack of clarity.

Oh. How thick of the fog, to be born that way.

It can't help it.

No? I thought it was its *nature*?

Never! The fog is too uncertain to have a nature.

Oh. *(Dismissing the subject:)* Let's go out into the sun.

Yes. All doubt is cleared away, under the sun's intense illumination.

Yes. You can carve it with a knife.

What?

The sun.

Wrong metaphor.

Oh. I'm so fuzzy-minded.

(Compassionately:) Poor kid. Your fog will clear up.

(Hopefully:) Will it?

Yes. Let's greet the sun.

Our Saviour! *(They walk in sun's window-beams toward door.)*

(Outside door entrance, drenched in pure golden sunlight that obliterates visibility in its own way as the fog did its own:) How dazzling! It's so blinding!

Where are we?

Indefinable.

Then we're in a fog?

Of sorts.

SPACE SHRUNKEN INTO TIME

The days hasten by. But we are faced with meanwhile.
Good old space! *That's* constant, and never varies.
Space is bigger outside than in. Let the window form the
border line.
And the shrinkage goes on. What occurs in the psyche?
Something contrary to astronomy. How narrow!
When space is this thin, it needs *time* to decide.
And when the individual concludes, is his death general?
Or only one window blinks out, while the skyscraper grows.

RELATIVE POSITIONS

(But how relative is only one point? It tends to be absolute, instead. Loyalty to its very self is even part of its very isolation, when considered not in relation to any point else. That's the point made, in this unspeakable play. Other points remain unmade: therefore unsaid.)

The straightest line between two points is if you run.

But what if you run *slow*?

That's not the point.

But there were *two* points: is it the other one?

No. It's the joint between them. In slow motion.

What if, though, crooked?

So much the less is it straight.

Is there a third point?

Not unless you appoint one.

I wouldn't be disappointing.

Nor *that* way pointing?

No. I'll line up straight, and shoot.

Shoot what?

Straight ahead. Then go back.

Back how?

To the starting point.

Where will *that* get you?

Out of line, again. Never mind at what speed. Running is only to bring two points together, as their link. When there's *one* point, the *accent*uation is on standing still, to reinforce the point. That brings fewer things into play, but makes running unnecessary. You see how geometry and physics-efficiency-economy arrive at the same thing, when only one is regarded? What an intensification of simplicity!

But to a dynamic sacrifice. Better to speed things up. You might err, but there's more to gain. *Two* points can *relate*: but what can *one* do?

Stagnate. While at a pause. It's running straight at itself, while never succeeding. That's why it's always there.

TWO PEOPLE ARRIVING AT THE SAME POINT THEY STARTED TO POINT OUT, YET THEY *DID* COVER GROUND. BUT *HOW*?

They say that the closest distance between two points is a straight line. But I maintain that the closest distance between two points is just *remaining* there.

Remaining there?

Yeah. Don't move. *That*'s the closest distance.

But you don't get anywhere, at the same time.

So what? Are you supposed to?

From one point to another. There's the distance. You postulated it.

Then *you* worry about it.

I will. If there are *two* points, where is "there?" You can only stay in the same place if there's only *one* point, to stay at. If there are *more* than one point, there's a *distance*. And to *negotiate* the distance, there's movement.

Is that so?

Yeah, I'm right.

Do you *stick* to what you say?

I don't budge.

And you've *made* your point.

My point is made; arrived at, determined, asserted; justified, defended, and maintained. Do you get my point?

I get it. It's *ours*, now, then.

But there's *two* of *us*; and only one point between us?

Does it disap*point* you?

No; I appoint you to be steadfast to it.

No point in not being so.

Good. We're there. Conversationally, we're at one. Bodily, we're separate, and apart.

That's a good point.

The same; but seen from a new tilt of angle.

Diverse angles converge toward the same point?

To *meet* there; or as angles, they're lost.

A RUMINATION ON THE DISTANCE OF TRAVEL

BY TWO MEN CONDUCTING ONE DIALOGUE

Is there the same distance between New York and Paris as there is between Paris and New York?

Yes, except for being the other way.

You mean once something is reversed, it's no longer what it was?

It's even the opposite.

But doesn't *distance* between remain constant?

Isn't distance neutral, unpartisan, about those two points it separates in common?

Points? Those are cities, living cities. Paris has been going on continuously for centuries, showing no signs of stopping, though all the while in the same place. There's never been a bigger French city in the whole world. Now as for New York . . .

I'm not talking about what the distance *connects*—but about the distance as a big body all incorporated of itself.

A big body at *that* size would need some feeding! No *wonder* the farms are wearing out!

Yet distance doesn't require food to keep itself alive.

How does it do it, then?

Through travel.

You mean the distance takes a trip?

No, but the distance is what the travelers pass over on, in their transports between those two cities.

Then the distance merely has the passive function of a rug?

No, it's vital—it *permits* travel.

How? By issuing passports?

No, that's what the countries do to their citizens. Distance is composed, inch by inch, of many a mile.

Are you telling me that distance has patience?

It builds itself up slowly.

What!? In *this* jet age!?

Not only fast jet airplanes negotiate that distance, but the cumbersomely more antiquated modes of passage like ships.

Of course, you could always walk.

The ocean is not safe for pedestrians.

No. I didn't mean walk on the surface of the water: I meant walking on deck of the safe ship—to take a little air and exercise.

That's good for the health.

Yes. But meanwhile which way is the boat facing?

Well, if it's facing east it must be moving that way and so it's going in the direction of Paris. It *left* from the New York port, on the left, and proceeds *right* towards Paris on the right. All maps would agree to that, provided the reality is correct.

All right. And who are the passengers?

You mean aside from the ship officers and crew?

Yes; in other words, who paid?

Ah! Now we're getting down to money!

It's inconceivable to conceive of distance without money.

No, because I have a free conception of that distance in my mind right now.

Yes, but you're not *getting* anywhere.

You mean I'm stationary, and have missed the boat? But I didn't *want* to take it. I want to stay *here*.

You have a perfect right to. A man has a right to do what he wants. But you're not spending any money.

I spend money in transportation to get somewhere. But I don't *have* to spend money just to stay here.

That seems unfair. The freedom to travel and the freedom to remain ought to be equal. Yet one costs money and the other doesn't.

Is that because of the exchange rate between French and American money?

Totally irrelevant.

I won't tolerate that insult.

Then don't. But there ought to be a tax for staying somewhere, equal to the sum you spend in being in transit. All of life, whether in motion or still, ought to be equally expensive. Then all parts of the world will become economically connected.

I call that false economy.

Call it what you will. It doesn't alter the facts.

What *are* the facts?

You want me to go into them *all*?

Well, digest them.

No, I already had my meal.

I mean select the high points.

They're the Empire State Building and the Eiffel Tower.

That still doesn't get us anywhere.

You call getting between New York and Paris not getting anywhere? You must be a rural chauvinist, to heap such contempt on commerce between giant cities.

Since when is traveling to be confused with commerce?

Since the tourist trade as set up, at mutual profit.

Mutual to whom?

To all concerned. Money changes hands.

Then money is being continually amputated to have its hands replaced.

It can always grow new ones from roots in the flesh at the wrist. Plus, there's a varied supply of transplants at hand.

That's handy. No wonder money is so grasping, with all those hands!

No, you're confusing money with *people*.

So were you.

That's understandable. People *use* money.

And they're used *by* money.

Same with distance. Distance uses the cities it connects; and is used by them, to get through, in case of travel.

Yes, distance is what's passed through.

One day, there will be no more distance between New York and Paris.

Why not?

The cities will merge.

Internationally?

If necessary, yes.

Where will the ocean become?

A dried river, with its Parisian and New York banks.

Will each bank bear its own rate of interest?

No, a mutual fund will be deposited in each.

Where will language be, once the world is unified?

Along with distance, it will be abolished.

How will people speak?

A lot, as always, what with their propensity to loquacity.

But via what words?

All words will be the one. As all places will unite their distances into one.

But what will happen to variety, diversity, the multiplexity of all separate individual things?

Into the melting pot. We'll brew a big stew.

With all things one, what will happen? There doesn't seem to be much room for travel. Thus eliminating transportation.

You go everywhere at once by remaining. It's all in the mind.

The world to impose no physical obstacles? All difficulty removed?

All space and time narrowed as one. New York in Paris, while *containing* Paris. Man liberated from the terror of distance, but deprived of the joy of discovery. He'll *be* where he could go, *already*: so no need to go, when you already *are*. Time barriers removed. Spatial boundaries conquered. Man having melted into the cosmos, as one man, in all things. The animal kingdom and the human race becoming one with vegetable and mineral ancestry. And everywhere, at the same time.

Sounds like a dream.

The dream today is tomorrow's fact.

I'm glad there's a division between us. I like being separate from you.

Yes. So let's keep this sexless.

RECONCILING THE TOO-CLOSENESS BETWEEN THE ELIMINATION AREA AND THE ROMANTIC-EROTIC ONE GEOGRAPHICALLY UNDER US, THROUGH A MENTAL ASSIMILATION-UNITY THAT LIFTS OUR BEING ABOVE OUR MERE PELVIC STATION AND PROVIDES ANATOMICAL SPIRITUALIZATION FOR INCONGRUOUS NEIGHBORS IN AN EVER WIDENING FRAME

Two contrary objects can be in the same vicinity.

You mean a slum tenement can be right next to a luxury apartment building?

Not only that; but the source of romance and the source of embarrassment can be anatomically very close together.

Are you referring to the bottom parts under, and frontal-under, the controversial region of people's pelvic area?

Blushingly, yes. The paradoxical meeting place. The grossly mismatched union, under our very bodies. Civilization compensates—or tries to—in its architectural domestic interiors, where the bathroom is a separate room entirely from the bedroom.

They're separate under our bodies too; quite distinct; but, compromisingly close together in breathless spatial juxtaposition. No tearing them apart.

Must we *live* under such conditions?

I don't know about you; but *I* live *over* them!

Don't get fancy, or high-and-mighty. You're putting on airs.

By use of the "below," I can put on *heirs*.

Below redounds with *numerous* hairs.

It's beneath us to refer always to that area, we're above what we are. *Consciousness* is our true station.

But with my *consciousness*, I *think* of what's below.

Then you're *above* what you think *of*.

But what I think *of* is beneath my thinking?

Yes, and your *being* is located in your *thinking*, not in your thinking's *object*.

I *am* my thinking?

So to speak.

Good. Then I elevate what I think *of*, to my thinking's eminence. And so my pelvic area is in my head. *Sublimated* so to speak.

Does it remain functioning, at your head's level?

Organically, I'm all at one. Everywhere, in me.

Good. Don't separate. Assimilate. Integrate. Be all that you do, in the unity at what you are, letting geography drift anatomically apart to an incorporate isolation.

Clarify your obscurity.

In obscurity is my clarity one complex whole.

WHAT CAN WE NEED?

Lots of flowers to have in the house; piles of bookcases; and other material possessions. Deep big windows, with showy views; exalted bathrooms, with tile and ivory; enchanted wall-paper; and the most modern of antique furniture, placed strategically along truly opulent rugs; and people in the house, too, to give it a human dimension. What could be lacking? Soul, spirit? No, plenty of nature outdoors, and a very private sky, dotted at intervals with the latest in cloud fashions. Here is a very heaven of money, in full demonstration! Wealth, put to full use, in dividends of current human happiness! God is redundant, with such a performance: the poor claim Him, lacking more substantial things.

WITHIN THE WORLD, THERE'S ME. AND WITHIN ME, IT—TO A REDUCED SCALE.

I want the world to be different than it is.

Well, then do something about it.

Me? I'm only one man.

Well, stand up and be counted.

People can count me with just one finger: that's all it takes.

But the world remains. What difference do *you* make to it?

A little. Just by being me.

And the world?

The world is plural. It's a gigantic plurality. However, I contain a replica of it—a tiny capsule reproduction of all its immensity—quite within me. A working model, I have—of the world, and how to get around in it, or around the problems in it, or over its numerous obstacles that crop up like overnight weeds. I've internalized this globe, history and all, as have my co-residents on it, and the globe is what's between us in common, me and my fellows. Its rhythm and social evolution are ours, as well.

Do you make a dent?

As a participant, I do. There are no spectators—we're all performers, in this thronged arena.

Aren't many things in this world repugnant?

Revolting! But I'm only me. What can I do?

You can do little things, locally, affecting some people.

Within my small orbit, I can. As far as it goes.

But things in their entirety—

Too immense. Too abstract, as well. Concrete particulars, within my domain, my province, my concern: those affect me. In turn, I deal with them.

But the universe is vastly out of range?

It dwarfs me entirely. I may not alter the course of things—save in my immediate vicinity, where I give small nudges. For my limits are immense. I'm hemmed in, by colossally universal limits. Modestly, they give me my brief space. This I gladly take—to make of it the bit I've done and will make. Before my so private death. My all-too-local death. My death of such terrific unconcern to my plural fellow men. As is, of course, my life. Save, in degrees, to just a few, who border on my own compass. I know them, to extents. My knowledge has a span. Within it, *all* is known. I touch *all* other spans, especially of those whom I'll never meet. In me, they rage.

ALL THE WORLD'S A PUN

After having punned all morning, I decided to shut up. It was
not easy. At first I succeeded, but gradually I failed. The afternoon
sun was hidden by all my puns, and the moon gladly accepted
eclipse, before the well of my puns ran dry, and sleep chased the
mind away. In the morning, new puns started. It was regarded
soon, that life was nothing but a pun, boiled down. Thus, I had
worn away all but essence; and in the beginning, I concluded
was the pun.

MARVIN COHEN

Moon Dragon Press   Broadside no. 1   New York City   1975

AFTERWORD: AT YADDO

[This piece is part of From Mt San Angelo, *a 1984 memoir by William Smart.]*

In the early sixties, when I was teaching at Skidmore in Saratoga Springs, New York, there was, out on the edge of town about a mile-and-a-half from the college, a mysterious place called "Yaddo." From the road all you saw were woods, and two large, stone gateposts on each side of the entrance drive. I don't recall if there were actual gates or a sign saying KEEP OUT-PRIVATE PROPERTY, but that was the feeling you got—that this was a very private and exclusive place, sort of like those estates in James Bond movies where secret agents learned the deadly devices of their trade. All I knew about Yaddo was that it was something called an "artists' colony" and that famous writers, artists, and composers came and hid out there from time to time. Occasionally we'd actually see one. Malcolm Cowley gave a talk at the college once, and I heard that *he* was out there, and that all the scruffy-looking younger men and women who came into the hall with him that night were also out there.

. . .

By then I think I was beginning to realize that Auden and Frost and Eliot weren't the only living poets in the world, that there might even be one or two I'd never heard of. Considering the fact that I was almost thirty years old and the Creative Writing instructor at Skidmore, this was a rather late awakening. On the other hand, it might still not have occurred if, about a year before, I hadn't met another writer from Yaddo, and this time got to know him fairly well during the month he was there.

I met Marvin Cohen at a reception for Hortense Calisher, who had just published a new novel. The reception was held at a coffeehouse in Saratoga called Cafe Lena where Yaddo peo-

ple liked to go to hear folk music and where, the previous summer, I had acted in a play. I had learned by now that whenever
you met someone from Yaddo, the first question to ask was simply, "What do you do?" and the Yaddo person would answer, "I
paint" or "I write" or "I write music," and you took it from there.
So:

"What do you do?"

"What?"

"What do you *do*?"

"Just a minute." He twisted something in his ear and I saw
he was wearing a hearing-aid, even though he couldn't have
been over thirty. "Say it again."

"I said, what do you do?"

"I write."

"What sort of writing?"

"Fantasies about my imaginary life. What do you do?"

"I teach at Skidmore."

"Oh, I thought you were from Yaddo. I just got here this afternoon."

"Where from?"

"The City."

He was wearing a black coat several sizes too big for him and
the knot of his tie was half-twisted under his collar. His shirt
was a green-and-orange flannel outdoorsman's shirt, but his
face was pale and pasty, as if he hadn't been outdoors in years.

"Where in the city?"

"Avenue C. You know it?"

I shook my head and said, "Only through Galway Kinnell's
The Avenue Bearing the Initial of Christ into the New World."

"What's that?"

"A poem."

"I don't read poetry."

A writer *who doesn't read poetry?* I thought.

He looked straight at me and said, "I bet *you* write poetry."

I shrugged. "A little."

"I could tell."

"How?" I asked.

"You just look like someone who writes poetry." He grinned.

"No offense!"

The next time I saw Marvin Cohen I was sitting in my office grading papers, and from down the hall I heard a voice asking my chairman, "Is there a guy named Bill Smart here?" I heard Joe give directions back to my office, and a moment later Marvin appeared in the door.

"I happened to be going by and saw the sign English House and figured I'd find you here." He looked at the papers on my desk and said, "Writing?"

"Grading papers," I said.

"You want to go get a Coke?"

It was spring, very warm in fact, but Marvin had on a long overcoat and an old hat, and the hearing-aid wire went from his ear down under the collar of his coat. I noticed girls glancing at him as we walked along the street. He had a strange loping walk, and his shoes slapped the pavement like clown shoes. After we had passed a couple of dozen girls, he said, "How can you stand it !"

"You get used to it," I said.

Marvin shook his head in disbelief and continued to stare at every girl we passed. When I greeted one I recognized from a class, Marvin said, "What's her name? Maybe I could call her up and get a date. You could fix me up. Tell her you have this terrific friend—say I'm a poet! How about it?"

That evening I told my wife about Marvin Cohen coming by the office and speculated on what my chairman probably thought. She suggested that perhaps I ought to say something in an off-hand way tomorrow about Marvin being from Yaddo and not anyone I knew. "You know how Joe is." I did indeed.

A few days later I paid my first visit to Yaddo, arriving precisely at the appointed hour and finding Marvin sitting on a stone wall next to a *porte-cochère*, like a toad on the palace steps. The house behind him looked big enough to have fifty rooms. Before I even got out of the car he said, "Did you bring something?" I nodded, turned off the engine, picked up the envelope lying on the seat beside me, and got out.

"You want to see the 'Italian Gardens'?" Marvin asked, and led me around the outside of the house and down a long lawn. At the bottom we walked around pools full of lily-pads and statues of nymphs and fawns. "Nineteenth-century decadence," Marvin said; then, "Who are some writers you like?"

It was so abrupt, I had to think a moment before replying.

". . . Hemingway . . . Faulkner . . . Fitzgerald . . ."

"F-f-f-*Fitz*gerald," Marvin shouted, stuttering for the first time. "Christ!" and explained for two minutes why Fitzgerald was such a bad writer.

When he was finished, I asked, "Who do *you* like?" looking for a chance to get even.

"*Cervantes!*" he said, and that ended that.

Coming back up the hill he pointed out the tower in which Truman Capote had written *Other Voices, Other Rooms* and sniffed to indicate what he thought of the history of the place.

"Are there any famous writers here now?" I asked.

"Philip Roth," he said, "another one of your Fitzgerald types." Then he glanced at me and said, "Instead of asking if people are *famous*, why don't you ask if they're any good?"

All this was so upsetting I was sorry I'd come and I'd be damned if I'd let him read my stuff. We walked up the lawn in silence. Ahead of us the house sat huge and impervious, all gray stone and windows that reflected silvery blackness.

"Want to see the inside?" Marvin asked as we reached some marble steps.

"Sure," I said, "but I can't stay."

"It'll be quick. We're not supposed to bring people in from outside. It's like *The Magic Mountain* here."

The interior was just what I expected—high, baronial ceilings, wooden beams, carved-wood chairs so big two could sit side-by-side as uncomfortably as one, a couple of nineteenth-century, Russian-looking sleighs, an enormous stained-glass window depicting some historical scene, and old sofas and armchairs covered in frayed velvet and damask.

"They say Edgar Allan Poe wrote 'The Raven' here."

"I wouldn't be surprised," I said.

"Come on, I'll show you my room," he said, starting up the stairs, "but don't talk. They're very strict about that."

As we turned at the landing, I whispered, "I feel like I'm being snuck into a dorm," and Marvin sniggered. Going along the hallway, I heard a typewriter being typed in the distance and wondered if it could be Philip Roth.

When we got to his room, Marvin took a key out of his pocket and unlocked the door. But when he opened it, I was surprised to see another door right behind it. It was like opening a door onto a boarded-up wall, like a cartoon without a caption. Marvin opened the second door, then closed them both behind us. "This took a while to get used to," he said. "I kept closing the wrong door first."

The room was huge and full of sunlight. There was a narrow bed and a spindle-legged writing table with a straight-back chair and an old overstuffed chair with a floor-lamp standing beside it. Through the windows I could see the gardens at the foot of the lawn. Marvin's coat and tie were hanging over the doorknob of what must have been the closet. On top of the dresser I could see pill bottles and a box of Saltines and two candy bars. Sitting on the floor beside the dresser was a cheap little canvas bag with a rip in the side and a piece of rope for one of the handles.

"What's it like, being here?" I asked.

"Too quiet. I miss hearing people being shot at night."

"God, what I wouldn't give for a room like this." I sighed, looking at his desk. "You should try writing on a card-table in the bedroom."

"I have."

"With a wife and three kids?"

"No, just my girlfriend sometimes."

"That's a little different," I said.

He nodded, then stepped over to the desk and picked up a large manila envelope. "Here," he said. "Tell me what you think."

I glanced down at the envelope. On the front was written

The Self-Devoted Friend

by

Marvin Cohen

When I looked up, Marvin was looking at the envelope I was holding in my hand, the one I'd gotten out of the car with.

"Listen," I said, "I've decided I don't want you to read it after all. I don't think you'd like it."

"Don't be stupid," he said. "You probably won't like my stuff either."

It was so unlike my own precious sensitivity, my Holy Devotion to an idea of art so high I could hardly finish a paragraph, that instead of withholding I simply handed it over and said, "Look, I've got to go," and started for the door.

"I'll see you out."

Again, as we went down the hall, we could hear a typewriter ratta-tat-tatting softly in the distance.

Back outside Marvin said, "Look, you can't call me here, so I'll call you sometime next week. Your number's in the phone book, isn't it? There aren't any other Smarts?"

"No, I'm the only one."

"Okay, I'll give you a call."

Driving out, down through the pines and past a little pond, I saw two women walking along the road. When they smiled, I smiled back, wondering if they were writers or painters or what. You couldn't tell anything about an artist just by looking. Most of them were very ordinary and unimpressive, hardly noticeable.

The next time I saw Marvin, a week or so later, he told me the piece in the *Kenyon Review* was clever in a nasty sort of way but everything else was too sentimental and romantic and why didn't I just write the way I talked. I said I couldn't, I took writing too seriously. He shrugged and asked what I thought of *The Self-Devoted Friend*.

"It's strange," I said. "Surrealistic. I *like* it, but I think there's a limited audience for that sort of thing."

"You're right!" Marvin said, and burst out laughing. "I may be the only one who likes it."

The last time I saw Marvin was near the end of his stay, one night when I got him to come to our house to babysit while my wife and I went to a party. My wife was a little nervous about leaving Marvin with the kids, but I told her he'd be perfectly fine, in fact they'd probably love him. And of course they did; when I picked him up at Yaddo he had a grocery bag full of Cokes and potato chips and candy-bars, and I suspect he even brought along the manuscript of *The Self-Devoted Friend* to read to them at bedtime. My wife, naturally, prepared a long list of instructions on each of their bedtimes, what snacks they could have, the number where we could be reached, and of course the numbers of the Rescue Squad, Police, and Fire Department. I'm sure she was very nervous all evening. But when we got back, they were all asleep in their beds and all the lights were off but a single lamp next to the chair in which Marvin was reading. He didn't hear us come in. (I had told him not to turn off his hearing-aid, but I assume he had: it was probably the only way he could read.) Anyway, everything was fine, I actually got out my wallet and paid Marvin the standard babysitter's fee, and as I drove him back out to Yaddo he recounted all the things they'd done. He said he'd expected hourly phone calls from the Rescue Squad, Police, and Fire Department, checking up, but everything had gone fine. And he had indeed read part of *The Self-Devoted Friend* to Paul (who was six then) and he thought Paul had liked it. "He's smarter than you, Smart," and we laughed.

"Marvin, I *like* it," I said. "I think it's terrific. All I said was it's too strange for *most* people."

"Well, I couldn't write the sort of stuff 'most people' like if my life depended on it."

In the silence that followed, all I thought about was Marvin's wonderful self-confidence and my own total lack of it, and how much I envied him. How much righter *he* was, and what a coward *I* was.

Then Marvin interrupted my thoughts by saying, "I really envy you . . . having a wife and kids . . . lots of friends . . .living the way you do. You should see my place, all the cockroaches, my mattress on the floor . . ."

"But you have time to write," I said.

"Yeah, well . . ."

I didn't want to hear anything that might disillusion me, so I changed the subject. Because I was turning into the gates at Yaddo, I said, "How's it been, being here?"

"Okay, it turns out." My car lights lit up an opossum crossing the road, head down, hairless nose and long tail, like a huge rat. "The time and silence don't mean as much to me as most people—I've got plenty of that back in New York—but I've enjoyed the dinners." I smiled. Marvin went on: "I like the company at dinner-time, and of course the food's a lot better than I usually eat."

"It'd be the opposite with me," I said. "What I need is the time and quiet."

"You ought to apply," Marvin said.

"I probably couldn't get in."

I hoped he would say "Sure you could," but all he said was, "You ought to at least try."

I pulled up behind the mansion. All the lights were out, it was totally dark. I thought about the twenty or thirty writers and painters and composers asleep inside.

"I hope they left the door unlocked," Marvin said. He went over and tried it and came back to the car. "Listen," he said, "let's get together sometime if you're ever in New York. I'll show you Avenue C."

"I'll try," I said, "but I never get into the city. You know how it is."

"Yeah, well, if you ever do."

"Right. And let me know next time you're here."

"Sure."

. . .

I never saw Marvin Cohen again. [. . .] Then, strangely enough, my son Paul, who's twenty-seven now, ran into Marvin at a party in Greenwich Village, and when he told him his name Marvin asked if he was related to a guy named Bill Smart who used to live up in Saratoga Springs? And when Paul said I was his father, Marvin said, "I babysat you! It's amazing! The only time in my life I ever babysat, and you survived!" and told Paul all the details of that evening and I'm sure asked him if he recalled *The Self-Devoted Friend*.

∞

[Note: When recently asked what he got out of Yaddo, Marvin replied: "some social life & romantic life & writing life, squeezed into 2 months. & the experience of being away from New York."]

Marvin Cohen at a Lower East Side exhibition opening, 17th November 2018.
Photo by Maggie Beale.

Marvin Cohen is the author of many novels, plays, and collections of essays, stories, and poems.

His shorter work has appeared in over 100 magazines and books, including: *Ambit, Antaeus, Assembling, Center Magazine, Cricket Addict's Archive, Essaying Essays, Extensions, Harper's Bazaar, Hudson Review, Monk's Pond, The Nation, National Camp Director's Guide, New Directions in Prose and Poetry, The New York Times, Plays from the New York Shakespeare Festival, The Pushcart Prize, Quarterly Review of Literature, Salmagundi, Sun and Moon, Transatlantic Review, The Village Voice, Vogue (UK)*, and *Wormwood Review*.

His writing ranges from the experimental to fable; from poetry to prose; from internal dialogues to playscripts; from art criticism to cricket fandom; from humour to philosophical essays, and from aesthetics to surrealism (he says "if people say so then it must be true").

His work has been performed on radio and theatres in the USA and the UK, including readings at the Poets at the Public Series, featuring, amongst others, Richard Dreyfuss and Wallace Shawn.

Born in Brooklyn in 1931, Cohen has described himself as one who has "risen from lower-class background to lower-class foreground." He studied art at Cooper Union but left college to focus on writing, supporting himself with a series of odd jobs, from mink farmer to merchant seaman. He later taught creative writing at various New York colleges, including The New School, the City College of New York and Adelphi University.

For a long time, Marvin Cohen has lived in the Lower East Side, New York City, with his wife Candace.

BLANK PAGE BOOKS

are dedicated to the memory of Royce M. Becker,
who designed Sagging Meniscus books from 2015–2020.

They are:

IVÁN ARGÜELLES
THE BLANK PAGE

JESI BENDER
KINDERKRANKENHAUS

MARVIN COHEN
BOOBOO ROI
THE HARD LIFE OF A STONE, AND OTHER THOUGHTS

GRAHAM GUEST
HENRY'S CHAPEL

JOSHUA KORNREICH
CAVANAUGH
SHAKES BEAR IN THE DARK

STEPHEN MOLES
YOUR DARK MEANING, MOUSE

M.J. NICHOLLS
CONDEMNED TO CYMRU

PAOLO PERGOLA
RESET

BARDSLEY ROSENBRIDGE
SORRY, I BROKE YOUR PROMISE

CHRISTOPHER CARTER SANDERSON
THE SUPPORT VERSES

www.ingramcontent.com/pod-product-compliance
Lightning Source LLC
Chambersburg PA
CBHW030650020726
47493CB00006B/1963